MEN A

Dominic Cooper has lived in London and Edinburgn, working at various jobs, and spent two years in Iceland. He is now settled on the west coast of Scotland. His first novel, *The Dead of Winter*, won the Somerset Maugham Award; it was described by C. J. Driver as 'hard, intelligent and passionate' and by Janice Elliott as 'one of the most powerful first novels I have read for some time'. In addition to *Men at Axlir*, his other novels are *Sunrise* and *The Horn Fellow*.

Dominic Cooper

MEN AT AXLIR

*A novel concerning the case of
Sunnefa Jónsdóttir*

HARVILL
An Imprint of HarperCollins *Publishers*

First published by Chatto & Windus, 1978
This revised edition first published in 1992
by Harvill
an imprint of HarperCollins Publishers
77–85 Fulham Palace Road,
Hammersmith, London W6 8JB

9 8 7 6 5 4 3 2 1

BRITISH LIBRARY CATALOGUING IN PUBLICATION DATA

Cooper, Dominic 1944–
Men at Axlir.
I. Title
823.914

ISBN 0 00 271127 3

Map by Vincent Driver

Set in Linotron Plantin by
Rowland Phototypesetting Ltd
Bury St Edmunds, Suffolk

Made and printed in Great Britain by
Hartnolls Limited, Bodmin, Cornwall

CONTENTS

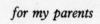

for my parents

FOREWORD

Sunnefumálid (the Case of Sunnefa) is a true story and a story well known to most Icelanders. But beyond the entries in the annals of the Assembly and the various, if completely different, versions of this incident that have appeared in modern times, few specific facts are readily available. In all the versions I read, names and dates predominate, while possible motives and final conclusions are, in the main, lacking. The book that I have written, I do not present as an historical novel but more as a novel based on historical fact.

Iceland in the eighteenth century – and, in fact, from 1380 to 1918 – was a Danish colony. As with all colonies, there were violent feelings between the colonists and the natives; but, in this particular case, I believe that the natives' complaints about their overlords were more than usually justified. The main cause for complaint was that a trade monopoly, which lasted till 1770, ruled that Icelanders were to trade only with Danish merchants. These latter, knowing themselves without competition, were often guilty of giving ludicrously low rates of exchange and of selling the people rotten produce. This in itself, when the general standard of living barely reached subsistence level, was enough to ensure that the Danes were hated.

It may help English readers to know that Icelandic personal names follow the system of patronymics. That is to say that if, for example, Jón Magnússon has a son called Eiríkur and a daughter called Anna, his children's full names will be Eiríkur Jónsson and Anna Jónsdóttir. The only exception to this system is that a few of the grander families, usually of Danish stock, took a surname. It is also worth noting that Icelandic women retain their own names when they marry.

I should like to thank all the many people in Iceland whose hospitality and kindness made the writing of this book possible and if I am not able to name them all individually, I should at least like to single out my very good friends in Reykjavík, Hrafn Hardarson and Anna Sigrídur Einarsdóttir, who were indefatigable with both advice and enthusiasm; and also to mention Jakob Gudlaugsson and Gudveig

7

Bjarnadóttir out at Skaftafell where this book was born. To them and to Don and Ann McAllester whose generosity with their house in Ardnamurchan helped in the actual writing of this story, my deepest thanks.

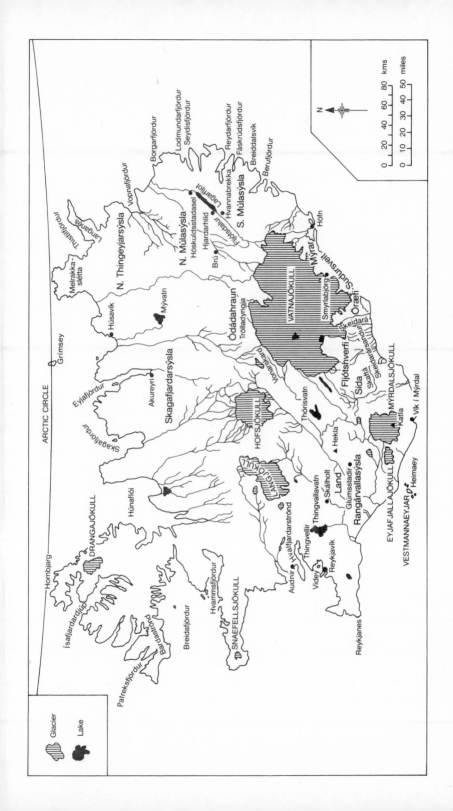

*. . . en systirin hét Sunnefa. Hún var talin fríðust kona
á Íslandi um þær mundir.*

. . . and the sister was called Sunnefa. She was
considered the most beautiful woman in the whole
of Iceland at the time.

Gísli Konráðsson, Huld

1

GUNNAR THÓRDARSON, DOCTOR (i)

The sound of Elise Rosenberg's ring striking against her crystal glass roused me from my fit of reverie. The conversation was as lively as ever but still harped endlessly on the same subjects – the price of butter, some new lace that had come out on the last boat from Denmark, the difficulties of convincing the farmers of the sudden scarcity of tobacco (they simply thought you were withholding it in the hope of getting higher offers) and the inexhaustible porridge of scandal, politics and intrigue that had found its way out to Reykjavík via the ships' captains and the occasional outdated news-sheet. Perhaps I could just take a sip of wine, make some passing comment and let them get on with it again . . . My age and the fact that I seemed to be able to carry off a singularly good impersonation of a man listening with interest would perhaps allow me to retire to my own thoughts without being dragged back into the conversation. All I had to do was to give an odd smile or nod here and there to maintain the decency of my silence. Me and my wine and the world going by – that was all I wanted.

That June night of 1804, there were eight of us at the table of Anders Rosenberg, Danish merchant, in the house up on the slopes at the back of the little town. The table was covered with crisp white linen. The best wax candles burned with steady, bright flames in their silver candlesticks so that countless little lights flared on the cutlery, the crystal and the Danish porcelain. Most of the food had been cleared away and we men pulled philosophically at cigars while Elise Rosenberg and the other women plucked small pleasures from the little bowl of sweetmeats that she had ceremoniously brought out for the occasion. Out through the window opposite me, the light of the midnight sun lay softly in the sky. Over the low island of Videy, its warmth rubbed gently up against the mountain flanks of Esja.

I sank back into my trance. But a while later there was a sudden lull in the conversation and I took my chance.

'Well, Anders,' I said, 'I'd best be on my way. I promised my sister that I'd be back at Audnir by the morning.'

'Gunnar!' cried Elise. 'You must be mad! I won't hear of it. How

11

can you think of riding all that way without any sleep? At your age! No, no, you'll sleep here tonight and we'll set you on your way tomorrow morning after a good breakfast.'

She tutted and shook her head in outrage.

'Seventy-four may seem ancient to a woman of your few years,' I replied laughing, 'but I've spent most of my life travelling around the country on horseback and a few extra hours won't do me any harm. At my age you don't need much sleep. And anyway, look!' I added. 'Look what a night it is!'

Everyone turned towards the window. Indeed it was a night of nights, breathless, with that strange flush of dusty pinkness hanging over the expanses of the sea where the headlands of Kjalarnes and Akranes rested lightly on the waters.

'May I ride with you, Gunnar? I've to go as far as Hvalfjardarströnd myself.'

Kjartan Hardarson was a tall, well-built youth of seventeen with brown hair, a large nose and slow eyes, who lived out at Bakki in Hvalfjardarströnd. His father was for ever inciting him to befriend the Rosenbergs' son in the hope that a close relationship between the boys might increase his chances of getting goods on credit at Anders's stores. But Kjartan had little time for the Danish boy's sickly ways and his patronizing fashion of speaking. He had only come for his father's sake that evening and for most of the time had done little more than maintain a deferential politeness.

'But of course, Kjartan. I'd be pleased to have your company.'

Elise tried to protest again and Anders sought to deflect me from my purpose by offering me some more wine. But by now I was filled with a desire to get away from this little Danish enclave and enjoy the summer's night. At my age, one could never count on another summer.

We all got up from the table. I said goodbye to the other guests and turned to thank the Rosenbergs. They stood side by side in front of the table smiling at me. They both had their hands clasped over the roundness of their stomachs; and with the glow from the table the picture was one of such fat comfort and security that I almost laughed aloud. With a warm house packed with fripperies and all the unneeded yet seemingly vital possessions of the wealthy, with an existence stretching no further that the slow-paced schedule of the trading boats, the bartering of goods with the farmers and the occasional social evening with the governor or one of the other

Danes, what indeed could one expect them to know of the country?

'Thank you for a most enjoyable evening, Elise.'

'It was nice to see you, Gunnar. Come and see us again soon. You've been out at Audnir for a year now and we've scarcely seen anything of you. You really mustn't neglect us so.'

'Ah well, at my age, you know . . . Goodnight, Anders!'

I walked out and went round the corner of the house to find Kjartan sitting silently on his horse, staring out across the sea to the west. It was quite light but everything was flat and dimensionless. The suggestion of a breeze rose from time to time as we rode away across the hill but it was more in the nature of a soft swell of slack air than a wind. The island of Videy lay before us like a sleeping whale. The horses' hoofs sounded out in odd rhythms as we passed over the changing earth. Rocks and moss and mud and crushed lava and sweet, sucking bog. Sheep stirred and rose in the flowery twilight and then were gone. Great clouds of fish-smells enveloped us, reminding us of the scattering of farms that lay at rest in the creases of the land. You could smell the sea too, sharp salt and sea-weed, making one always think of the hundreds of miles of cold water that separated us from the world. The world? Iceland and the world? Yes, that is how it always seems to us.

We rode at a fast pace for some way, shaking off the headiness of the Rosenbergs' party. We rode in silence too, our only contact the occasional touching of our legs as the horses found their way through the rocks. I glanced at my companion from time to time and the night's light showed a heavy-browed, stern face that stared out over his horse's head. I smiled to myself remembering the boundless angers and indignation of my youth. Ah! I thought, ah, indeed . . . ! The young man's fervour, the old man's complacency. What an ancient story!

'Well then, what was it really like?' he said aggressively.

'What was what like?'

'What they were talking about at dinner . . . the time of the Skaftá Fires.'

'Why ask me?' I replied roughly, frowning and setting my horse into a fast trot that quickly left him behind. He caught up with me a moment later, breathing heavily, and said more calmly:

'Well, I'd an idea that you were in the south when the eruptions took place.'

We rode on.

13

'I was,' I said eventually. 'I was in Sída when it started.'

A great heaviness filled my mind. Suddenly, the softness of the summer night was splitting open around me with the old horrors. I felt an ineffable exhaustion at the memory of those years.

'Was it that bad?' asked Kjartan, watching me with fixed eyes.

'Bad?' I whispered. The horses climbed slowly up a slope. 'Yes, it was bad . . .'

We stopped our horses at the top of the rise and sat facing each other.

'And then you were out in the east before you came to Audnir?'

'Yes,' I replied distractedly. 'I arrived there in '85. The previous doctor had died. And I stayed there until I retired last year.'

'And where exactly were you in the east?'

'I had the doctor's house at Skógargerdi on the Lagarfljót.'

'Did you ever see Sheriff Wium then?'

I looked at him sharply. His face was fierce again.

'Yes, I knew him.'

'Then why did you speak up for him when Anders mentioned him this evening? That man Wium was a bastard!' he said passionately.

A little rag of wind scuttled between us. I smiled sadly.

'Young men have always been readier to follow their passions rather than the facts.'

'Are you speaking of Hans Wium?' he asked sheepishly.

'No,' I said with an involuntary sternness. 'I'm speaking for the moment of you.'

He looked down.

'But everyone knows what he did to that wretched girl and her brother.'

'Kjartan,' I replied, 'one day you'll learn that nobody knows anything for sure. Hans Wium died fifteen or sixteen years ago when you were only a year or so old. How can you possibly say that you know the truth about his life?'

He did not answer for a moment but rubbed his eyebrow with the heel of his hand.

'Do you know then?'

My momentary anger began to drain away like the backwash of surf, leaving me flattened and sad. I thought of that last year of Hans's life out in the east, of the countryside crippled by the ash, of the people dead or weakened near to death, and of my long talks with Einar in the small room at Hjardarhlíd with the dying man next

14

door. It was a distant world and one which for years now I had been trying to crush from my memory. I thought too of Pétur, deranged and bitter to the last, locked away in his loneliness at Hvannabrekka under the steep hillside where the snow and ash hung in fields of dirty pallor. And again of poor Jón, a pathetic giant gnawed by confusion and despair when I had last seen him those long years ago in Land . . . But I had come into the story too late. I had seen this, heard that, listened to Einar's account of all he had witnessed and heard – but, even then, there were gaps, gaps that could now never be filled, for the people who might have known what really happened were gone. Had I the right to say categorically that I knew the truth?

'No, perhaps I don't know for sure either . . . It was foolish of me to speak like that.' I paused, feeling humbled and no longer certain of myself. 'But, you know, it's wrong of people to speak of Hans Wium like that, saying that he was a criminal. Perhaps he was a bad man, perhaps much of what has been said about him is true. I myself don't believe so. But nobody really knows and in my way of thinking there's no place for judging men in that way . . . If I had to say what I believe was the case, I should say that Hans was basically a good man – weak, God knows, like all of us, but good in that his life was ruled by compassion.'

'Compassion?' exploded Kjartan. 'Where in God's name was the compassion in what he did?'

I sighed. A coat, a heavy silver ring and the feverish words of the dying man . . . What right had I to defend him?

I turned my horse and set off again.

'What a night!' I cried, suddenly moved once again by joy. 'Do you ever have the feeling at times like this that you are newly born, that your memories of living are merely stories you overheard somewhere?'

Kjartan laughed quietly by my side.

'Yes,' he said. 'Yes, I do.'

'Let's ride slowly,' I said warmly after a moment, 'and I'll tell you what I know of Hans Wium . . . It was after the Skaftá Fires, in the summer of '85, that I arrived at Skógargerdi . . . But no, if you're to understand how things were during my first years in the east, I'd best go back a bit and tell you of the Fires.

'Ever since 1754 when I got back from studying in Copenhagen, I'd held the job of doctor to the whole southern part of the country. It was an impossible business. I did what I could but there was

15

hunger and disease everywhere, and the people often all but losing their minds in their struggle just to survive. It's hard to know quite how they managed to keep going.

'You know, Kjartan, these past hundred years have been nothing but a procession of disasters for us. Back in 1718, there was the smallpox epidemic that killed off about a third of the population. Then a whole series of violent eruptions that brought us down even further. By 1730 – the year I was born – there was a complete state of famine. For most of my childhood it went on like this; and even when I got back from abroad, little seemed to have changed. In fact, during my first six years back home, it was said that ten thousand people died, of mere starvation. When Katla erupted under the ice, the floods were devastating; and later, in '66, Hekla erupted and that eruption went on without a break for two whole years. Yet, unbelievably, there was worse to come.

'In 1782, the winter was severe, with long, hard frosts and snow lying much deeper than is normal in the south. As usual, we tried to get by as best we could and simply prayed that the spring wouldn't be too late in coming. As the winter moved into its last months, we could think of nothing but the coming sun and that miraculous moment when the ice would start to break loose.

'March passed into April and our hopes rose in aniticipation. But then April had become May and while the sun rose higher and higher into the sky, the frosts and snows continued. Before we could fully understand what was happening, the time of spring had gone and the so-called summer months were with us; but each morning the earth was still as hard as the rocks and the snows lay as deep as ever. And then we were overwhelmed by a sullen despair, that depthless despair that only comes after ruined hopes . . .

'That year there was to be neither spring nor summer. In early June, there were reports of drift-ice fifteen miles off the south coast; and in the north there was dense sea-ice right through until mid-summer. And, of course, with weather like that there was virtually no growth of grass so that the harvest produced only enough hay for a handful of beasts. Our diet consisted in the main of mountain moss, angelica roots and sea-weed. And so another thousand people were dead. It'd been the coldest summer in living memory . . . I needn't tell you how the families with young children felt as they watched the days begin to shorten and the new winter come stealing into the sky . . .

16

'But somehow we got through that next winter. And our hearts lifted when eventually the thaw came and the grass began to show itself fresh and green. In April, an eruption began out to sea in the south-west, off Reykjanes, and a new island appeared. We laughed light-heartedly at this, making jokes about how our country was growing. It was the laughter of relief, relief firstly that the summer would soon be on us but also that the eruption had happened far away. We could rest a bit. There wouldn't be another eruption so soon afterwards. Oh, sweet Jesu, what irony!

'In the third week of May 1783, I left Vík í Mýrdal – where I was living – and went east across the desert of Mýrdalssandur to visit the farms in Sída and Fljótshverfi. The weather was bright and clear. The farmers and their wives were full of good spirits saying that at last the good Lord had seen fit to give us easy times after all we'd been through. And so I went about my work . . .'

I paused, all of a sudden overcome by the memory of that summer. My chin slumped on to my chest as the horses slithered their way down a muddy slope to a stream. Kjartan took hold of my elbow.

'Are you all right?'

'Yes, yes . . .' My heart was pumping. My mouth was dry.

The horses crossed the stream and bucked and stamped up the opposite bank. From where we were on the flat ground at the back of Gufunes one could see the opening of the valley leading up to Mosfell under Esja. There was not a sound to be heard other than the shushing of the horses' hoofs in the grass. Everything was held by peace and the mystery of the northern night.

THE SKAFTÁ FIRES

Forty miles across the desert of Mýrdalssandur, over which Gunnar Thórdarson passed on his way east from Vík í Mýrdal, the small farm of Skál stood by itself under the slopes of the hills. Looking back westwards over the river Skaftá, the farms of Skaftártunga could be seen lying dotted about in the folds of the rough sheep-land. Eastwards, more farms ran in an irregular chain through the hamlet of Kirkjubæjarklaustur and the districts known as Sída and Fljótshverfi until they reached the massive bluffs of Lómagnúpur. Beyond Lómagnúpur there was nothing for twenty-five miles, noth-

17

ing but the flat blackness of the sands where countless rivers, large and small, twisted and battled their way from the outlet glacier of Skeidarárjökull to the sea. Unless one chose to go inland and creep across the edge of the ice, this desert was as often as not impassable for its rivers were deep and fierce and vilely cold. To try and ford them was to throw oneself into the hands of providence. Who knew how the river-bed had changed in the few days since the last crossing had been made? Somebody you had met had bragged that he had just come west over the great river, Skeidará, without too much bother – so you might take your chance, perhaps only a day or two later, at the very place he had told you of . . . But then perhaps your horse goes a yard or so north of the first man's route, stumbles into a deep hole, gets knocked down by the current and there you are in the tumbling waters of mud and melted ice. Perhaps – again – your horse is lucky and a good swimmer so that he manages to struggle across and find a place among the ice to get out. Perhaps not. But for sure, you with your heavy clothing can only thrash and gasp for a few seconds before the cold hamstrings your strength or a rock stuns you and your good wife no longer has a husband to fend for her . . . No, for most people, for most of the year, the cliffs of Lómagnúpur marked the end of the road east. The district of Öræfi, on the other side of the sands, could have been in another world.

On the afternoon of Sunday, June 1st 1783 – Gunnar told Kjartan – he happened to be at the farm of Skál. He was sitting outside on the grass with the farmer's family, enjoying weather which they had not had for two years.

All of a sudden, there was a dull, cavernous growling sound from behind the hills and the ground began to tremble, a light tremor that lasted only an instant. For a moment nobody spoke. Then one of the old men said 'Blessed God . . . no!' and the woman called sharply to her daughter.

At that moment the second tremor came, growing quickly from a light shaking to a pitch of violent rocking and hammering that threw every one of them to the ground. The sound of things falling in the farmhouse could be heard over the rumbling and cracking of the earthquake. Everything seemed hazed and unfocused: even the sun was springing about in the blue, summer sky.

When it had finally passed, they lay there poised for the next onslaught.

'Lord in heaven, let that be all . . .' somebody whispered.

Eventually they collected their things and crept into the house, almost as if they feared that any sound might set it all off again. The house – three turf and stone buildings run together – had its back wall formed by the hillside. Its outer walls were thick and though pieces of turf and dried moss had been shaken loose from the roof, the sturdy structure appeared not to have been damaged.

Up the valley of the Skaftá, little clouds of dust and grit could be seen hanging loosely in the air – but apart from this, everything seemed just as peaceful as it had earlier in the afternoon. Yet when one of them set off to check the animals, he came across long, thin cracks in the ground.

All through that still, quiet afternoon and evening they were filled with dread at the thought that there might be more to come. And indeed, shortly after midnight, as they lay sleeplessly in the big beds, the earthquake started again. Not as fiercely as before yet persistently, in a series of attacks that went on and on until the early morning.

During the following week there were no further shows of force. The sky clouded over and remained low and leaden for several days with a strange brown or purple hue to it. Twice one of the younger men tried to ride west over the Skaftá to get news from the farms beyond but on both occasions he found the river vastly swollen with more than seventy fathoms of water to cross at the place they normally used. Some of the farmers from further east in Sída came over to Skál but while there was much smoking and discussing, nobody had any specific news to give.

At the weekend the weather cleared. On the Sunday morning – it was Whitsunday – the sky was cloudless and a light breeze, coming in off the sea, ruffled the thick grass on the farmhouse roof. Gunnar was helping the men saddle the horses for the ride to church when they heard a tremendous explosion out in the hills to the north of Sída. The women came running out to see what had happened and found them all staring back over the farm in amazement. Rising up from further inland was a vast plume of smoke and dust that, even as they watched, began to spread in all directions. Other explosions sounded out and moments later new discharges burst up into the cloud so that in no time at all the whole of the sky over Sída and Fljótshverfi was swamped by it. A short while later the ash began to fall.

Huddled together inside the farm, they tried to make light of the

19

eruption so as not to frighten the little girl. But the explosions grew more and more frequent until there was a steady booming and banging as the noises resounded in the hills. The ash-fall was constantly increasing and, as the minutes went by, the light began to fail. By midday it was quite dark indoors while outside there remained only a murky light in the drizzle of ash. And in the evening, the earthquake started again.

All next day there was nothing but blasting and darkness. At one moment, in a sudden horror of being trapped in the farm, one of the men rode out and picked his way down to the Skaftá. The river had almost vanished: at the bottom of the bed was a little gush of water no bigger than a mountain stream. In the half-light and with the tremendous noises at some ungauged distance up the river valley, the scene was so eerie and unnatural that he could not bring himself to ride across and so just turned his horse and made for home.

That night there was a cloudburst and the following morning a number of heavy showers so that the ash – which by now covered every inch of the ground – was turned into a grey, gritty mush. But worse than this were the acrid gases that followed the rain, gases that made everybody struggle to get their breath and that all but killed one of the old men with his weak chest. And as the smell of the gases got stronger, they all began to complain of a smarting sensation in their eyes and on the exposed parts of their bodies. When Gunnar went out to try and find some clean drinking water, he came back saying that he had seen burn marks on the plants and even on the sheep.

And so the day passed and another night came, bringing with it an increase in the noise, as if the ground to the north were slowly splitting open in the direction of the farm. Somewhere around breakfast time (it was now almost impossible to judge the hours of the day), a cold wind blew up from the east and dried out the mushy ash, hardening it into a crusty, shell-like growth on the ground.

Closeted indoors with nothing but their own thoughts and with their nerves shredded by the unbroken sounds of the bombardment, Gunnar and the others began to feel that they would go mad unless they could find out what was happening. So Gunnar and the farmer put on gloves, wrapped blankets round their heads and, improvising masks to protect their faces from the burning airs, rode off in the direction of the river. The horses constantly whinnied and snorted and rolled their eyes.

20

As they got near to the river, the noises became deafening. The river, as before, was virtually non-existent and as they rounded a small knoll they finally saw why. For in the canyon where the waters normally ran stood a vast wall of lava, a fifty-foot-thick flood of liquid heat, red and orange and faced with pock-marks of blackness as scabs of clinker tumbled and were pushed in slow motion by the pressures of the ever-growing masses upstream. The river that rose in the glacier forty miles away, that gathered a thousand smaller rivers and streams to itself and that, for centuries, had poured in a broad flood down past the farms, had now been knocked aside overnight by this monstrous, glowing growth. The waters must still have been pouring off the glacier and the streams off the hills – but of them there was no sign.

Though it moved slowly, perhaps no more than five or six yards in the hour, the lava's relentless advance, accompanied by clouds of smoke and noises like cannon and drum, held the two men paralysed. They sat there, staring in horror through the slits of their masks, and dumbly realized that as the lava came out of the constriction of the canyon, it was spreading into a broad tongue which would eat up the grasslands where the farm's best sheep were grazed. And they saw too that if the flow continued, it would inevitably creep round the base of the hills towards the farm itself.

But as they sat there peering through the thick light, they suddenly caught sight of a man on horseback across the river who was waving to attract their attention. They rode out over the empty bed to meet him.

'Are you all right at Skál?' the other man, similarly clad, shouted through his mask.

'Yes, for the moment,' answered Gunnar's companion, 'but it looks as if the fires were turning our way. How about you?'

'Not so good. I lost my mother last night – poor old thing simply couldn't get enough air. The rest of us are all right, I suppose, but the young ones are frightened out of their wits . . . Young Kristinn and Sverrir, Hjálmar's boys over at Hóll, went north yesterday to try and see where it was all coming from. Apparently it's a good way off – about twenty miles in, up at Úlfarsdalur. They say the fire-mouths stretch in one long line across the hills north-eastwards: but it was hard to make out because of the poor light and the steam from where the fires struck the river . . .' He paused for a moment, choking for breath. 'What are you going to do?'

'God only knows. But if it keeps on in the same direction, I'm done for – that's my best land out there. And anyway we'll not be safe at Skál if it gets any nearer. But how are things with all the others in Skaftártunga?'

'Well, the five farms up the valley have all gone under and a couple more were in such danger that they had to be abandoned. We've got the people from them down with us at the moment.'

'God! If only the bloody air would clear! You can't breathe, you can't see. The wretched beasts will never stand it.'

The man from across the river nodded and then the three of them just sat there, no longer shouting to make themselves heard but letting the fire-flood's clamour pour over them.

On the way back to Skál it began to rain. They looked up at the sky and were puzzled. For the rain was more than rain, it was water mixed with grit and thin slivers of light stone that prickled and prodded at their bodies like blunt needles. And as before, the rainfall brought renewed waves of gases so that both of them were soon sick and dizzy, and their eyes pouring with tears.

While the strange rain passed over quite quickly, the gases became gradually stronger and early that night, after choking and gasping for several hours, the old man with the bad chest died, just as if he had been slowly throttled. The little girl vomited and retched all through the evening till she was so weak that she could no longer stand. They wanted to try and give her milk but the cow had gone completely dry in spite of all the grass they had cut for fodder. So they tried some fish broth instead but the girl only cried and spluttered and brought it all up again. Later, when they lay dozing in their beds, they were roused by dull thuds against the door. Lighting the little fish-oil lamp, Gunnar peered cautiously out of the door and found a merlin and two redwings lying half-dead, stunned and crazed by the poison. At the edge of the light thrown by the lamp, other birds flashed and scuttered wildly in the thick, dark air. But even as he stood watching them, Gunnar heard a cry and hurried back into the house to find the woman staring at the corpse of her daughter.

And all the while, the thudding and booming grew steadily louder.

*   *   *

In the following six weeks, the eruption continued unabated. The flow of lava, bursting forth from the bed of the Skaftá, then split into three tongues, the largest of which poured straight on until it formed a great smoking sheet far out over the flat lands towards the sea; while another one advanced towards the farms of Skaftártunga, putting all the people to flight. Beastlike, it engulfed the little homesteads one by one and pressed on across the edge of Mýrdalssandur as if sniffing out the farmlands away to the south.

Meanwhile, as had been expected, an eastern arm rounded the base of the hills and made on towards the farms of Sída. And it moved so fast that the people remaining at Skál had to leap up in the middle of the night, seize a few belongings and escape with the horses and what livestock was at hand while the groaning snout of the fire edged remorselessly on behind them. When they rode back the next day, they found the farmhouse still intact though only yards above the lava which had buried the sheep-pen and the turf hut where they smoked the Christmas mutton.

At the end of July, the long line of vents up in Úlfarsdalur suddenly doubled in length, so increasing the line of fire-mouths to a length of fifteen miles. At this, the flow coming down the river valley dwindled but, to everyone's horror, a new one appeared some twenty miles further east. For the next seven months this second flood was to come grinding and smoking down through the hills, finally crossing the belt of farms and heading on southwards so that the people of Fljótshverfi – with whom Gunnar was now sheltering – found themselves virtually cut off from the rest of the country, trapped between the fire and the desert of Skeidarársandur.

And so it was that while the fires continued to rage, the evil summer passed away and the cold began to return. But news slowly began to come through that it was not only the south that was in desperate straits: for the vast cloud of ash and gas had spread across the whole country, stunting the growth of grass.

And as the year moved into its darkest months, the temperature continued to fall, bringing unparalleled frosts and snows. For months on end the frost lay biting into the ground while the fjords were closed off by sea-ice. By the end of that winter, in April 1784, it looked as though the country were doomed. Here and there, an occasional cow staggered about in a dazed and moribund state; but nearly all the sheep and horses were gone and those that had somehow survived were no more than skeletons. There were even reports

23

of horses driven to such extremes of hunger as to eat the carcasses of their own kind.

The people themselves were in no better state and had only maintained a flicker of life in their frozen flesh by digging up old fishbones from the midden to boil them in gruesome concoctions in which roots and dogs played a major part. When these plain commodities also failed, it became a common enough sight to see men and women chewing sheep's horns in the search for sustenance.

But these desperate efforts were never enough for men whose existence at the best of times was precarious. After the eruptions and diseases of earlier years, the combined assault of the past winters and the fires in the south proved too much and the death-rate went on rising. With no horses to get the dead to the churchyards and with the ground in places frozen to a depth of six feet, it soon became normal practice for communal graves to be dug between the farms. The dead were carried or dragged through the snow to be piled into these ugly holes; and with blizzards and sleet and murderous winds hampering the burial parties, it sometimes happened that one of the workers would also breathe out his last chill breath and fall in with the bodies of his family and neighbours.

All over the country the population was rotten with disease. There was the flux that literally drained them; the scurvy that made their hair fall out and their gums swell and burst; pneumonia, bronchitis and a hundred other ailments that covered them with boils or mange and racked them with agonizing swellings of the joints. Reduced to this level of existence, some of them turned to murder and pillage though this brought them little profit for there was almost nothing left to steal. Other men, in the madness of their despair, abandoned their wives and children to wander off over the countryside begging: but more often than not they were found again when the winter snows finally thawed, and usually only a mile or two from their homes.

But eventually the spring did come. And when it came, the Skaftá Fires were over. The lava had taken two churches and thirteen farms with thirty other homes in the area badly damaged. But, bad as this was, the fire was nothing compared with the ravages that the poisonous cloud had wrought throughout the country. Now, once again, there was quiet in the land: but it was the quietness of death – the country's martyrdom was still incomplete.

For those past ten months the people had seen neither the sun

24

nor the moon, other than as dim blobs showing through the bluish haze that lay over the island. For those ten months they had lived through their trials in a poisoned twilight, half-dead people drifting about in a half-dead world. And now that the winter was over, it was the clear sunlight and the warm breezes that were needed. But the light and warmth never came. As some of the ports began to open with the dispersal of the sea-ice, a few ships appeared from abroad with food and supplies but the run on these goods was such that prices surged out of control. In any case, the farmers, who rarely dealt in money, had nothing to sell in exchange for the food; and so all the merchandise went to the handful of men in the better positions. The rest of the population were expected to make the best of things . . .

The new year wore on and if there was no sign of the sun and its blessed warmth, they were at least thankful to have escaped the rigours of winter.

In the summer, there were new earthquakes and the land was filled with strange signs that put fear into the people and led them to believe that the end of the world was approaching. Bogs and marshes dried up, streams turned white and hot springs that had bubbled and spouted for centuries died, while new ones appeared in unexpected places. Unheard-of beasts showed themselves in the lakes and fjords and vast cracks that were said to be bottomless opened in the earth.

Early in the following year, in the middle of yet another iron winter, news came out from Reykjavík that the governor, Stefán Thórarinsson, had been informed by the minister in Copenhagen, Hans Kristoffer Didrik Victor von Levetzau, that the Danish government was considering the evacuation of the whole Icelandic population to the uninhabited parts of Jutland. While the Danes wrangled over the cost of such a move, the people of Iceland, even in their dire condition, spoke in anger and indignation of this plan. It was as if the Danes, who for centuries had exploited them through stringent trade monopolies and casual tyranny, simply regarded them as a herd of beasts that could be moved to better grazing. In the event, however, it was deemed that the cost would be too great – and so the Icelandic nation was graciously permitted to struggle on.

'Here, have a drink,' said Kjartan.

'Thanks. What is it?'

'Corn brandy. Anders Rosenberg gave me it for my father. I'm sure the old man won't mind if we give it a try.'

We drank from the little leather flask and smiled at the way the spirit clawed us in the throat. We drank again. My mind was opening out once more from the darkness of the blue haze and the ash. I closed my eyes and rolled my head back to the sky, breathing in the glassiness of the air.

'But you got by in the end?'

'Oh, we got by all right . . . We always do, don't we?' I could not keep a note of bitterness from my voice.

'So you went east to replace the doctor then?'

'Yes . . . You see, the ships that'd first come in to the fjords in the east had not only brought food: they'd also brought us another dose of smallpox . . .'

'God! What a time for that to come!'

'Precisely. Anyway, old Björn, the doctor up there, was one of the first to go. So I left my assistant in charge and went east to take over. I came round from Vík í Mýrdal to Seydisfjördur, which was where the disease had started. Christ, what a mess the place was in! I stayed there a month or so, doing what I could, and then moved inland to the doctor's house . . .'

We fell silent. But after a while, as we rode leisurely up the valley below Mosfell, Kjartan reminded me about Hans Wium.

'So it'll have been during the famine after the Skaftá Fires that you first saw him.'

'Who?'

'Hans Wium.'

'Oh, Hans . . . Yes, it was right in the middle of the bad times, when I first arrived in Múlasýsla, that I met him.'

'He'll have been an old man by then, I imagine?'

'Hans? He must've been in his early seventies – but he looked a good deal older. He was not a happy man.'

'And was it from him that you heard about Sunnefa's case?'

'No, I heard most of it from Einar, who'd been his secretary since

Hans got his first post as sheriff in the Vestmannaeyjar as a young man. But I also got to hear things elsewhere – from Gudný, Hans's sister, and from Sunnefa and Jón themselves.'

'You knew them too?'

'Well, I can't really say that I knew them well – but I certainly met them both.

'But, listen, if I'm to tell you the whole story, you'll have to bear with me. You see, no one person was actually involved throughout, so I heard much of it from quite different sources. But in those last years that I was at Skógargerdi, I used to sit and think about it all and try to imagine just how things had really been.

'Well, now, it was in the spring of '88, about two-and-a-half years after I'd come to Múlasýsla, with the country still pinned down by the ash and the famine and the smallpox, that I was witness to the last stage in Hans Wíum's tragedy . . .'

Kjartan nodded slowly.

'Here, have another mouthful.'

And again we drank together. The light of the dozing sun was already beginning to swell at the valley's head.

2

AN EPILOGUE: 1788

Although it was May, no birds sang in the valley and the wind was chill. The world still lay crushed by the ash and famine and disease that had followed the great fires in the south. That day, the only sounds were those of the wind, the small river and of the two horses that came with drooping heads and leaden hoofs up the track. Occasionally one of them would snort and shake its head or a hoof would ring out on a piece of rock: but mostly their progress was accompanied by nothing more than a numbed plodding.

The second of the two beasts was a pack-horse whose reins were tied to the tail of the horse in front. It was less a horse than an imitation of a horse for its ribs stood out as clearly as the teeth of a woman's comb while its belly bulged abnormally; but wretched beast as it was, it sufficed to carry the large leather and cloth bags that hung from its pack-saddle.

The other horse, though also in poor condition, was noticeably stronger and seemed to bear its burden with less difficulty. From any distance, it would have been hard to discern the sex of its rider if it had not been for the rough, wooden-framed, woman's side-saddle that it bore. For the woman had drawn the thick, black shawl around her head against the wind and sat hunched down in the saddle, and so presented nothing more than a formless bundle of blackness that gave little sign of life other than swaying with the movements of her mount.

She had been something of an enigma to the captain of the boat that had brought her out to Iceland. In the first place, it had seemed inconceivable that anyone should be choosing to return to the country at such a time of hardship. That in itself was strange. But when the person was an old woman and travelling alone, it could only be concluded that there was something queer afoot. And then again, when the captain had asked her where she was headed for and she had replied 'Fljótsdalur in Múlasýsla', he had suggested that he put her ashore in Reydarfjördur since she would be bound to find people there who were going through to Fljótsdalur with whom she could ride . . . This had seemed mere commonsense – but no, she had insisted on landing further to the south, in Berufjördur, and even said that if this were not convenient for him, she was quite prepared to pay him extra. He pointed out that it would be much more difficult to find horses in Berufjördur and that the chances of there being somebody to accompany her through to Fljótsdalur from there were very small. But, quite undeterred, she answered that horses could always be acquired if the price were right and as for riding alone, that would not worry her at all. But did she know the route through from Berufjördur? It was a rough climb up from the fjord and then there was a bad stretch of very lonely, high ground under Öxi . . . Yes, yes, she knew how it was – she had ridden that way before . . .

Once ashore in Berufjördur, she had tried to find some horses but, as the captain had warned her, was told that there were none for sale in the district. She, however, then mentioned a sum that had sent the man running to get a couple of his own horses. And while he was away, she had taken some coins from her baggage and put them in a small purse; so that when he returned, she was able to pay him and make the necessary despairing remarks and so give the impression that the coins were her last – thus avoiding being set upon by the greedy-eyed man and murdered for money which he might have suspected she had and which, in fact, she did have and in much larger quantities than he thought.

But not wishing to tempt providence, she wasted no time in getting the horses loaded and riding out of the district. She followed the fjord inland and then started up the long haul from the sea towards the narrow pass. Once on top, she had travelled in the most dismal conditions, picking her way in the thick cloud from cairn to cairn over the ash-covered ground. She was frightened up there in the wet, ominous clouds and her imagination made strange and horrible things out of the odd noises that she heard in the mist. But she was kept busy following the route for it was only roughly marked and when she had told the captain of the ship that she had ridden that way before, she had omitted to add that it had been all of forty-five years before, as a young girl of twenty, and on an occasion when she had been so frightened that she had scarcely noticed the countryside.

At last she came down out of the clouds and on to a busier track where she soon fell in with a family on their way north. For the rest of the day she shared the road with them, riding down a long valley that would eventually bring them out on the southern bank of the

29

Lagarfljót. That evening they put up at a farm; and the following morning, rising early, she set out alone and crossed over the hillside to come down through low woods to the edge of the Lagarfljót.

From this point onwards, her passing attracted more attention, for the track she was following led eventually to a dead-end, beyond which there was nothing but a wilderness of mountain and marsh and the great ice-fields of Vatnajökull. People, angry and aggressive in their hunger and weakness, stood and stared from their doorways. Others raised their heads from shoeing a horse or sharpening a knife and turned an enquiring eye to their companions. Children got up from the mud and came over to the track to stand and watch her go by. And when she had passed, there was much whispering as everyone speculated as to who this solitary woman might be. Of course, the further she went along the road, the fewer were the farms to which she might be going; so that the speculation increased as she progressed. But then, in the early afternoon, a man riding in the other direction brought back the information that not only had she continued on the road beyond the southern end of the Lagarfljót but that she had been seen to ride on up Sudurdalur. There were only two houses in Sudurdalur – the ramshackle small-holding where there lived Páll and his nephew; and the house at Hvannabrekka where Sheriff Pétur Thorsteinsson lived. And so it was summarily decided, with dumb nods and pursed lips, that she must be on her way to Hvannabrekka – for what could she possibly be to do with poor Páll? But the question still remained – who on earth was she? For not that many of them could even recall the days when anyone other than the sheriff had lived at Hvannabrekka – other, that is, than old Gunnlaug, the woman who had brought up Pétur. But Gunnlaug herself had been dead some fourteen years now . . . and, in any case, she had been an orphan, so it seemed most improbable that the passer-by had been anything to do with her . . .

The woman, meanwhile, had not been particularly aware of the interest she aroused, for she had been looking round with horror at the countryside's devastation. The fertile valley of the Lagarfljót, where the turf houses crouched under open, rounded hillsides, now showed only a pathetic resemblance to the landscape she remembered. Up on the rounded tops of the north-facing hills, the snow still lay deep; but the high whiteness only served to offset the black grit that was everywhere else. In places where the wind had thinned the layer of ash, new grass could be seen pushing bravely

30

through; but overall, the growth was miserably thin. She thought back to how the grass had been in her childhood, how every blade had been needed to fatten the sheep – and she trembled for the people.

The further she rode the more familiar the farms became and she stared in disbelief at what had become of them. In many cases, she took them for derelict, the dry-stone walls of small sheep-pens lying crumbled and scattered; doors swinging on broken hinges. Water pouring from the hillside across the turf roofs had turned the ground below into a morass; and carcasses of sheep littered the home-fields. And the farmhouses themselves showed no signs of being inhabited, not a wisp of smoke coming from the roof-openings. But then, looking back after she had passed, she would sometimes see a pallid, pock-marked face peering from the doorway.

At last she came to the end of the Lagarfljót. Here, through a long section studded with islands, the lake was fed by the river Jökulsá that came pouring down a narrow valley from the distant glacier. It was across this belt of islands that the river was normally forded. She stopped for a moment with the wind coiling about her and stared through the opening in her shawl at a large stone and wood house that stood on the slopes across the water by a collection of turf farm-buildings. The look in her eyes was one of anger and sadness. She started to ride down to the ford but then stopped abruptly and, wheeling round, urged her horses onwards.

The river Jökulsá flowed down the more northerly of two parallel and narrow valleys which were separated by a high, prow-like headland, edged with crags, that was called Múli. These two valleys were called respectively Nordurdalur and Sudurdalur.

Having hurried away from the ford, the woman settled her horse back to a slow walk and set off up into the mouth of Sudurdalur. Here a smaller river rushed along beneath the layered crags of Múli, adding a coldness to a landscape that was already chilled by the streaked ash and snow above. On both sides, the slopes were steep and high, the ash-covered grass cut by long falls of scree. Here and there a scrawny sheep could be seen nosing about but otherwise there was little sign of life.

But half-an-hour later, by now some time in the middle of the afternoon, she came upon a low building below an overhang of rock where a cave had been fenced off to form a sheep-pen. A couple of horses standing nearby suggested that the place had not actually

31

been abandoned. She dismounted and walked over to the building. She stood outside for a moment, listening, and then half opening the door, called out in a small voice.

'Hello! Is anyone at home?'

There was no reply and she was just about to walk in when something moved in the darkness and a hoarse voice called out.

'Go away!'

'Who's that?' she replied, stepping forwards.

'Go away!' said the voice more insistently. 'I've got the pox on me.'

The woman sprang back to the doorway, covering her face with her shawl.

'Who are you?' she asked.

'Kristján. And who are you?'

'But where are the others?'

'Others? What others? There are no others now. My uncle Páll was the last one to go and I buried him four days ago . . . But what's all that to you? Who are you anyway?'

But already the woman had turned and was gone, hurrying across the wet ground to her horses. She mounted quickly and rode off, driving the horses hard until they were out of sight of the building. Then, as she stopped to regain her breath, she saw, far out ahead of her, the farm of Hvannabrekka.

From a distance, it was just as she remembered it. It stood in a patch of flat, good land right at the head of the valley, with cliffs of a domed mountain rearing high above it. Even on a bright summer's day, the steep, rough hillsides and the barrier of rock and grass made Hvannabrekka an enclosed and menacing place; but now, seen under grey, flat skies with tatters of ash and snow draped about the upper slopes, the feeling was one of such brooding melancholy that there seemed to be an animosity in the place. And as she sat there gazing about her, it began to rain – a light rain but as cold as sleet and whipped about by the wind.

She put her head down again and the horses jolted forwards, splashing their way through a glassy stream that ran off the hill. The distant farm was now swept by veils of blown rain, was swallowed and regurgitated and swallowed up again. The wind was rising, changing from a cold but fitful breeze to a squalling force that sent sharp noises through the rocks. She hurried forwards, wanting to be home. Hvannabrekka home? She smiled weakly at the way she had suddenly thought of it as such. But now she could no longer see the house. She looked up at the clouds. It would probably be snowing on top. She had forgotten the precariousness of the Icelandic spring.

And then, quite suddenly, she found the house beside her. It grew out of what she had taken for a mass of rocks; became, in a brief shifting of the rain, the very place she had travelled so far to re-find.

Having seen how the country stood in the aftermath of the years of disaster, she had not really hoped to find Hvannabrekka just as she had left it; and yet, for all that, she had somehow not been prepared for the miserable state of decay and decline in which she now found it.

The house, built of stone and wood, was single-storeyed, though a window high in the gable-end gave light to a loft. On each side of the door and its small porchway, plain, square windows completed the simple architecture. But the white paint that had originally given the building an air of vigorous brightness among the stark hills was now chipped and peeling, and the windows were clouded by mud and grime.

Nearby, among the farm buildings, the ground was a dark quagmire of churned earth and water. Relics of the farm littered the ground, the rusty blade of a plough stabbing the water, piles of sodden sacking rotting among the rope-ends and tools that seemed to have been dropped in a moment of sudden apathy. In one of the doorways, where the lintel had collapsed, the weight of wood and turf hung down and a constant dribble of water spilled into a pool below. Here and there, the roof-timbers had rotted and given way so that pits and gaps had appeared in the turf roof.

For a while, she sat there on her horse with the rain gusting about her and her thoughts went back to that bright, windless day when last she had seen the place. At last, she urged her horses on and rode out into the mud. The beasts sank to their hocks and then to their knees as they floundered across, with the mud spattering her clothes.

She rode up to the door and, unwilling to climb down, kicked it several times with her small boot. The sound echoed dully and then vanished, leaving her in the silence of the rain. She looked round at one of the windows and saw a face hastily withdraw from sight. She waited, thinking that the person might be coming; but when no further sound was heard in the house, she kicked the door again, violently, as her anger rose. Then she heard a slight shuffling and

33

the sound of bolts being pulled back; and a moment later the door creaked open a few inches. A tall, white-haired man was peering suspiciously at her.

'What do you want? Are you clean?'

'I . . .' Her voice died as she stared at the face, grey and lined, and the small, polished eyes that watched her intently.

'How many times do I have to tell them we can't take in anyone else? Why does that fool of a district officer keep on sending people here? I'm sorry, you'll have to go back and ask for some other place.'

He was just about to close the door when she started to stammer something again.

'I . . . I was wondering . . .'

'Look,' he said, turning back to her and blocking the doorway, 'I can't make myself any clearer, can I? There's no room here. We've less than enough to get by on as it is. If we had another mouth to feed, we'd all end up starving.'

But she just sat there with a dumb, blank face, her mouth slightly open and her eyes filling with tears as she gazed at him. Disconcerted, he looked away and cast a glance over her pack-horse.

'Where are you from then? You're not from around here, are you?'

The rain had increased and was now pouring down, kicking up spouts of muddy water in the pools. It had penetrated her shawl which hung about her like a black, heavy shroud and ran in rivulets across her face. She raised a hand to wipe it from her eyes and her lips trembled. For a moment, she stared at him again and then spoke, almost under her breath.

'Pétur!'

'What's that?' he cried, now on edge from the woman's strange behaviour. 'Why do you look at me like that? I don't know you, do I?'

She smiled.

'Wasn't your father Thorsteinn Sigurdsson?'

There was a long silence before he spoke, his voice almost reduced to a whisper.

'Who are you?'

'And your mother Kristbjörg Ragnarsdóttir?'

'Woman, you worry me. My parents are long dead.'

She nodded slowly.

'Yes, of course. It was all so long ago. And the times have been

34

hard. But in those days you used to have a cousin, a young girl who loved you dearly . . .'

The old man, suddenly shaking all over, stepped forward into the rain and grasped her cold hand as it lay on the edge of her saddle.

'Yes,' she said slowly with a tired smile, 'yes, I'm Sólrún Haflidadóttir.'

And the wind, squalling down off the frozen heights, came tearing across the turf roofs and fell upon the trembling cousins.

*   *   *

Could it really all be starting up again?

Einar Eyjólfsson blinked and looked up at the oil-lamp. The soft light glinted on his half-glasses and created flickerings of fire across his watery eyes. He pursed his lips and looked down again. He had hoped to see Gunnar, the doctor at Skógargerdi, and talk to him about the whole matter; but Gunnar had warned him that his work up in Vopnafjördur to the north might keep him away longer than he planned – so it could be another week before he was back. And who else could he talk to? The others knew all about horses and sheep and their empty bellies but as far as talking about ideas and feelings, anything that one couldn't actually see or touch, well, they wouldn't know where to begin. And, in any case, on this particular subject he'd be the last person they'd speak to.

For the past twenty years or so, Einar thought to himself, things had been peaceful enough; and though Pétur Thorsteinsson had never missed an opportunity to cause trouble for Hans, the two men seemed to have accepted the stalemate in their enmity. And then, three weeks ago, that woman had appeared at Hvannabrekka and word had gone round that she was claiming to be Sólrún Haflidadóttir. The strange thing was that everybody had apparently accepted this without question though, so far, there had been no explanation of where she had been for the past forty-five years. But it was since the news of her arrival that things had begun to change at Hjardarhlíd. Initially, Einar had not taken much notice of Hans's behaviour for he was used to him being fractious and crotchety; but later he had become so jumpy and ill-at-ease that it had gradually conveyed itself to the other people about the house. So that now there was an odd feeling of unrest, of some inexplicable expectancy at Hjardarhlíd. Nobody actually said anything about it – least of all

35

Hans – but everybody sensed it. Which of them would have been prepared to say just what it was that made them catch their breath when a door slammed in the wind; or what, on still nights, made them seem agonized with indecision as to whether they should talk loudly to cover the silence or sit quiet in order to listen for . . . to listen for what? The sound of somebody approaching? And why was it that Hans had moved his desk round so that his back was against the wall and he could look out of the window opposite? And if there was no obvious reason for this, was it sheer coincidence that this window gave a clear view of the track coming down from Sudurdalur to the ford? Good God, wasn't that all over and done with now? It'd been going on for seventy years . . .

Einar stretched, extending his arms slowly so that he could feel the condition of his body. The action showed up his small, bony physique which was rather like that of an underfed boy. Only his hands were developed so that they looked overlarge in comparison, though they had a certain nervous fineness to them. His face, with the sharp-ridged nose where the glasses perched, was shiny and red with dry skin that flaked white around the hair-line.

He got up slowly, feeling all the aches and weakness of his seventy-eight years, and drank a glass of water. Then he walked over to the window and stared out at the thin darkness. There were certainly odd things happening these days. Why he had suddenly thought of it again, he was not sure; but he found himself wondering about that strange business with the shirt that had taken place a couple of weeks ago.

It had been a dark, windy evening and he had been sitting by the kitchen fire with the old woman who did the cooking at Hjardarhlíd when Hans had come in, wanting to know how there was mud on his bedroom floor when he had expressly forbidden anyone to go in there. The whole thing seemed rather unimportant, but Hans had been quite unreasonable about it. No more was thought about it until the following morning when he then wanted to know what was the meaning of the shirt he had just found under his pillow. He held up a filthy, tattered garment but nobody had any idea whose it might be – let alone how it had come to be under the sheriff's pillow. Hans angrily hurled the shirt on to the fire and walked out. The whole business had struck Einar as very odd . . .

He stood by the window for a while longer. Then, taking off his grey serge jacket and his shoes, he crept under the damp blankets.

He lay there on his back in the darkness, listening to Hans moving about restlessly in the next room. Finally he fell asleep and dreamed of himself as a cragsman on the fulmar-cliffs in the Vestmannaeyjar, the islands to the south where he had been born.

He awoke with a start. He glanced over at the window and saw that it was not yet fully light. What had woken him? He lay there listening and a moment later heard a long moan that sounded loud in the still, dawn silence. He got up quickly and went along to Hans's bedroom. He stood there in the silence and was just about to go back to bed when the groaning started again.

'Hans?' he called nervously.

'Einar?' The voice was muffled. 'Send somebody over to Skógar-gerdi. I need Gunnar.'

'He's not back yet. What's wrong?'

There was no answer and the groaning began again. He started to open the door.

'Don't come in!' cried Hans in a pinched voice. 'I think it's the pox.'

Einar closed the door again, his heart beating fast.

'Are you sure?'

'Yes. I know the symptoms. One doesn't forget.'

But Gunnar did not get back from the north until two days later, by which time it was clear to them all that Hans had indeed caught the smallpox. He had already passed through the primary fever with its profuse sweating, vomiting and the dull pain in the back; and on the third morning the evil redness broke out on his forehead. Andrés, a man who had come through a bad bout of the disease the previous winter and was so considered safe, undertook to be the person who helped him. Einar himself could do no more than look in through the open door at the large old man lying propped up in bed.

When Gunnar got back, he rode straight on down to Hjardarhlíd. As soon as he had washed his hands and stood by the fire to let the smoke cleanse him, he explained to Einar that Hans had got what the doctors called confluent smallpox. There were no signs of the prodromal rashes or the small spots of extravasation that normally appeared on the lower abdomen and the inside of the thighs and the eruption was entirely confined to the face. They would know for certain in a matter of hours, he explained, for the normal disease broke out in isolated pocks while the eruption in confluent smallpox

37

was all run together, bringing the facial skin up into large blisters. Einar, following the general drift of these technicalities, nodded solemnly and asked if this confluent smallpox was worse than the ordinary strain of the disease. The doctor replied that, as far as they knew, it was merely an intensified version of common smallpox.

'What are his chances then? At his age, I mean . . .' asked Einar.

'Small,' replied Gunnar.

Gunnar, thinking in terms of the whole district's health, wanted to know where Hans had been in the last fortnight. When he heard that he had been busy at his desk and had hardly set foot outside the house, Gunnar asked if anyone had been over to Hjardarhlíd to see him. But Einar replied that Hans had asked not to be disturbed; and so Einar himself had dealt with the handful of people who had come on business.

'Well, that's very strange,' mused the doctor. 'He must've caught it from somebody or something – and all the farms in the district are clear at the moment. Except for Holt, that is. Old man Páll was well on his way and his nephew Kristján had started it too. But that's the only place . . .'

When Gunnar came back the next day, he told Einar that there was no longer any doubt about the disease and that unless a miracle occurred, it could only be a matter of a week or so before the end.

As the days went by, Einar stood at the door of Hans's bedroom and watched the old man's face begin to swell and blister. In his youth, Hans had been a large, heavily built man with clear, green eyes and indomitable good spirits. He had had a fiery temper, especially when the drink was on him; but, at the same time, could be charming and generous with people. It had been an impressive sight to see him ride off to the district assemblies, a big, powerful man with a laughing face, sitting squarely on his well-saddled horse, and calling back to his companions in his high spirits. Yes, that was how it had been in those first days at Hjardarhlíd . . . And now, there he lay, grey-haired and shrunken, with dull eyes and the horrible mass of pocks turning into clusters of bulging, fluid-filled vesicles that gave his face the nightmarish look of a toad.

They fed him on weak broth and ewe's milk, kept his room darkened and covered his face with tepid compresses in order to try and relieve the burning of which he perpetually complained. Andrés told them that he constantly asked him to look out of the window and tell him what he saw. Andrés thought that Hans, becoming aware

38

of his approaching death, wanted to be told that the world was still alive, to hear how the snows were going, how the grasses were growing, how the countryside was gradually slipping into the soft, light days of summer: but when he started to try and cheer him up with such descriptions, the sick man impatiently cut him short.

'What else do you see? What else do you see?'

'Why, nothing in particular. The weather seems . . .'

'No, no – not that! What else? Surely you see something?'

They took it for the onset of the secondary fever which often brings delirium to the point of coma; but it seemed it was not this, only a marked increase in the fears and unease that had haunted him in the weeks before he had fallen ill. And then, one sunny day with a high north-easterly ripping spindrift off the Lagarfljót, this insistent questioning explained itself.

'It's bright and sunny today, Hans.'

'Do you see anything in particular?'

'Not much really . . . There's a man on horseback beyond the ford.'

'What's he doing?' Hans's voice had tightened.

'Why, he just seems to be sitting there – looking across this way.'

'Who is it? Who is it?' he said, his voice rising.

'Well, I couldn't rightly say . . . he's some way off.'

Hans started to raise himself up in the bed and threw back the bedclothes, his eyes bulging.

'Here now, Hans, you don't want to be doing that. You need to stay put.'

Hans sank back, gasping, and said in a low, hoarse voice:

'Andrés, I must know. Tell me who it is. You know all the men round here.'

'Well, if I had to put a guess to it, I'd say it was Sheriff Pétur Thorsteinsson.'

'Oh God!' The cry came out as if a thong were being slowly drawn tight round his neck. 'Oh God! What more does he want?'

'Nothing, nothing, I'm sure. Now just you lie back and I'll get you a bowl of milk.'

The puffed and suppurating head fell back on to the pillow.

That evening Gunnar told Einar that Hans was just beginning the final and worst stage. The smell in the house had become overpowering, a sweet, rotten smell as the fluid in the pocks had begun to putrefy. In some places the taut skin had burst and the pus oozed

39

down over the man's face. There was little that could be done for him other than cleaning his skin with a soft cloth but Gunnar, fearing that the secondary or suppurating fever was at hand, told Einar that he would stay the night in case it were necessary to give the patient chloral to calm the delirium.

The two men sat in Einar's room talking quietly as the daylight filtered away. Gunnar smoked continuously in an attempt to keep the smell at bay. Einar sharpened his quills. It seemed that, at last, the old, old story, the story that had lasted all those years, was nearly over.

JENS AND THORSTEINN: 1718–40

In the central section of Múlasýsla, the administration of the county was divided between the two sheriffs whose jobs gave them certain farms and the two best houses in the area – those at Hvannabrekka and Hjardarhlíd, both in the district of Fljótsdalur.

In 1718, the sheriff at Hvannabrekka was Thorsteinn Sigurdsson, a man of forty-three who had come to Múlasýsla a few years earlier after a period in a similar post up in the north. He was a dark, moody man of medium height and heavy build who wore a light beard to cover a rather unprepossessing chin. He was aware of his short-comings and though he despised himself for his moods and indeed tried hard to combat them, he was always considered a man who had to be humoured – and so was avoided. Because of this and because he in any case preferred to keep to himself, he never acquired any real enemies just as he had no close friends. But although this suited him in many ways, it also caused him much sadness for he believed in the brotherhood of man and would dearly have liked to feel himself accepted by the men and women who lived around him. However, since this was not to be, he contented himself with working hard at his job and, through exercising a scrupulous fairness in his dealings with people, felt that he was demonstrating exactly that concern and comradeship in which he so fervently believed and which he was unable to enjoy in his ordinary relationships with them.

In 1714, when he was still up in the north, he married a woman some fourteen years his junior. But to his dismay he found that their relationship never got beyond a certain friendly formality; and with his introverted tendency towards self-deprecation, he soon concluded that he was incapable of the love and affection necessary for a good marriage.

A short while after they had moved to Múlasýsla, however, his wife died in childbirth. The boy, Pétur, was brought up in the main by a young girl called Gunnlaug Kjartansdóttir who had been orphaned in the great smallpox epidemic of 1707. She was a good-looking girl of eighteen at the time of Pétur's birth and, having been eyeing the brooding sheriff for some while, she stepped only too willingly into the mother's shoes – initially only as a nurse to the child but later, when the nights grew cold, also as a solace to the lonely father. Thorsteinn found comfort with her but no more. Middle-age and the years of isolation had drawn a cordon round him. He turned once more to his work.

It was soon after this, in the spring of 1718, that Jens Wium moved into the sheriff's house at Hjardarhlíd with his wife and small son. He had come out from Denmark some years earlier to act as deputy to the king's agent at the trading station in Reydarfjördur. He was a tall, ruddy man with a large, soft face and a loud voice. Rumour had it that some criminal involvement had obliged him to leave Denmark.

Although Jens Wium was a Dane, Thorsteinn Sigurdsson resolved not to let the fact of his nationality come between them. For the past three hundred years or more the country had been under the rule of the Danes and Thorsteinn knew that there was nothing to be gained by crossing the Danish sheriffs. They had a name for being high-handed and extortionate; but it was virtually impossible for the Icelanders to contend with them for the Danes could always get matters referred back to the Supreme Court in Copenhagen, where verdicts were inevitably one-sided. Since he and Sheriff Wium were going to have to work together, it would be best to avoid any confrontation – those, at least, were Thorsteinn's thoughts as he rode down the valley from Hvannabrekka that day in the spring on his way to greet the new people at Hjardarhlíd.

But the relationship between the two men never stood a chance. However much good will the open-minded Thorsteinn might have shown, it could never have been enough to compensate for the domineering, bullying character of Jens Wium. From that first day, he treated Thorsteinn as a mere bumpkin and maintained a manner

41

that was offensively patronizing. Thorsteinn, being thirteen years older than the Dane and having experience in the job of sheriff, thought that he might be able to give Jens some ideas on the problems of running the district; but Jens simply talked through him. He kept making references to his royal ancestry (it was said that his mother had been the niece of Juliana Maria, the Danish queen), talked volubly about the clubs and social life of his native Copenhagen and spoke with quite undisguised scorn of everything Icelandic.

Ingibjörg Ingimundardóttir, his wife, whom he had married during his time in Reydarfjördur, was a tall, gentle-faced woman who seemed to move in a trance, like a bird before a snake, whenever her husband was present. She thought that most of Jens's bragging and aggression was only some kind of bluff – but it was beyond her to see that the large, garrulous man was, in fact, curiously unsure of himself. And while she, as a wife, may have forgiven some of Jens's rudeness and heavy-handed behaviour, Thorsteinn Sigurdsson certainly did not and he rode home that day angry that he and his country could be treated so.

But the difficulties between them did not remain confined to mere differences of opinion and attitude. Both the work and the fixed proportion of the revenues in the district were meant to be shared equally between the two sheriffs: but it soon became clear the Jens had no intention of sharing either. He took it upon himself to divide up the work and the profit as he thought best. He applied himself vigorously to all matters from which there was a good chance of financial gain and simply handed over the rest to Thorsteinn. To begin with, Thorsteinn, intent on the efficient running of the district, tried to ignore this. But when, later, he began to realize that the Dane was not only being unreasonably demanding and harsh on the farmers but was also embezzling the taxes – then a sullen and unquenchable anger erupted in him.

When he first got to hear of all this – some eighteen months after Jens had taken up the post – he considered the matter for a while and then rode over to Hjardarhlíd. He knew what the outcome of the visit would be before he got there; but felt that for his own peace of mind he must at least try to reason with the man. He broached the subject gently, in a roundabout way, keeping his eyes on Jens the whole time. The Dane sat there in silence, looking bored, but finally interrupted him and asked bluntly what he was trying to say.

At that, Thorsteinn angrily accused Jens of being both a tyrant and a thief. Jens sprang to his feet and shouted at Thorsteinn to get out of the house.

For months after that, Thorsteinn sat up at Hvannabrekka staring down the valley and wondering how he could put a stop to Jens's corruption. Once he had got over the row at Hjardarhlíd and had looked at things more dispassionately, his desire for justice was quite genuine. But as the days went by and he found himself repeatedly having to swallow his pride in his dealings with Jens, his motives began to change. Now real hatred began to blossom within him; and it grew until he could think of little else but bringing Jens down.

The fires were lit. But he knew that the only possibility of exposing Jens's crimes was to bring an irrefutable charge of embezzlement or general malpractice against him at the annual meeting of the Great Assembly at Thingvellir. But this would have meant producing firm evidence to support his case – and this he could not procure. For the farmers, mainly simple men inured to endless hardship and exploitation, were frightened of Sheriff Wium. Without this specific evidence, the case would never stand a chance at the Assembly where Jens's prowess as a speaker would quickly have confused the whole issue.

As things stood, Thorsteinn saw that there was no way of touching Jens. His only hope was to be patient and wait for him to overstep the mark: it was bound to happen in the end – and Thorsteinn, with the single-mindedness of the embittered, was prepared to wait. And so the years began to roll past.

But for all that Jens seemed to Thorsteinn to be enjoying the fruits of his tyrannies, all was not well at Hjardarhlíd. His arrogance and his scorn for the people in his charge came back on him, ensuring that he had absolutely no companionship outside his own family. Though Ingibjörg was a good wife to him, she knew nothing of life outside the small confines of her own experience. When her husband spoke of all the things and people that had filled his youth back in Denmark and which he now clung to in his isolation and insecurity, she could only smile. And soon she had heard it all. Thus Jens, like Thorsteinn, was a lonely man.

In addition to young Hans, who had been born in Reydarfjördur, Ingibjörg bore two more children, both girls. The first lived only eighteen months before being taken by the flux; but Gudný, born in 1722, grew up into a pert, bright-eyed girl. But Jens cared little for his children, regarding them mainly as something to keep Ingibjörg occupied. For in the years following Gudný's birth, a distance had begun to grow between Jens and Ingibjörg. And with Jens away in the district for long periods at a time, the two children's lives soon came to be centred entirely round their mother: the large, loud-mouthed man whom they knew to be their father drew only the obedience of fear from them.

Ever since his student days back in Denmark, Jens had been prone to savage bouts of drinking. For a while, during his time in Reydarfjördur and the first months at Hjardarhlíd, he managed to contain this need. But as time went by and the isolation in which he lived began increasingly to bear down on him, so the drink started to reassert itself once more.

But any pleasure there was in drinking alone at Hjardarhlíd, under the silent, falcon eye of his wife, soon began to pall. Before long, he was making regular trips over to Hartman, the trader at Björnshús in Reydarfjördur; and since this was too far for the return journey to be made the same day, he took to making the most of his visit and spending three or four days there before coming home red-eyed and tetchy to Hjardarhlíd, where his wife said nothing yet walked around with the air of a martyr. These trips to Hartman and later to another Dane, Brønsted, up in Borgarfjördur, took place once or twice a month – otherwise his drinking was done in the solitude of his study at Hjardarhlíd while his wife lay sleeplessly in bed.

While Jens drank, Thorsteinn watched. When they rode out together on business, they rarely mentioned their home lives. Thorsteinn, though not a drinking man himself, would bring a bottle of brandy with him on their rounds and, in a feigned spirit of fellowship, would offer Jens a drink. Jens, staring with hard, beady eyes at the proffered bottle, was loath to let the Icelander see his weakness. But Thorsteinn would press him, laughing, as if Jens were hesitating through shyness – and in the end, Jens, with a false casualness, would accept. Thorsteinn would pretend to take a drink or two from the bottle before handing it back to him, telling him magnanimously to keep it as he had more back at Hvannabrekka. Which was perfectly true: and it was drink bought in for the sole purpose of supplying Jens's habit.

Thorsteinn's son, Pétur, a tough little boy with a shock of coarse hair, was growing fast. He was still too young to understand what was going on between his father and Sheriff Wium; but he caught the atmosphere between the two men and knew that, for some as yet unexplained reason, the people at Hjardarhlíd were enemies. Whenever he saw Hans Wium, he would turn away proudly and have nothing to do with him. Hans, a year older than Pétur, had no idea that there was anything odd in the relationship between the two families and so just shrugged his shoulders at the other boy's stand-offishness.

It was in 1731 that Thorsteinn took in his wife's niece at Hvanna-brekka. Sólrún Haflidadóttir from Thistilfjördur was a spirited girl with long, black hair, whose laughter and gentle mockery brought a dramatically new element into Pétur's life. At fifteen, he had developed into a sombre youth, a clear reflection of his father's bitterness and taciturnity; for Thorsteinn had already begun to fill his mind with his own hatred of the Wiums. It was grim material for a boy's life and the arrival of the eleven-year-old girl with her extrovert nature was a timely distraction from the morbid obsessions of his father.

On reaching the age of sixty, Thorsteinn decided that he could no longer afford to wait for Jens to incriminate himself. All along, he had continued to believe that the farmers, finally incited by Jens's behaviour, would approach him for help; or that the king's steward would notice something amiss in Jens's accounting and ask him, Thorsteinn, to investigate the matter. Yet somehow this never happened. But when it was rumoured that Sheriff Wium was thinking of appointing a deputy, Thorsteinn at last thought that his chance had come.

There was a man called Jón Bjarnason living at Gerdi in Álfta-fjördur, in the southern corner of Múlasýsla. He was a man whom Thorsteinn had had up before him on a charge of murder some years before. He had acquitted him for lack of evidence, though there had been little doubt in his mind of the man's guilt. Jón was a small, shifty man whose ruthlessness suggested that he was an ideal applicant for the work which Jens would have for a deputy.

Early in the summer of 1735, Thorsteinn rode south to Álfta-fjördur to see him. He found him living on his small farm with a slovenly woman and a number of ragamuffin children. After they had talked for a while, Thorsteinn asked him if he was content with his life as a farmer.

'Well, it could be worse, I suppose,' replied Jón.

'So how do you like the idea of a change?'

45

'A change? Depends what to.'

'I've heard Sheriff Wium up in Fljótsdalur is looking for a deputy.'

'And why should you think that that'd interest me?'

'Well, I'd say you could be doing a good deal better for yourself than you are here.'

'So would Sheriff Wium pay well?'

'No, I don't suppose so. But I would – to the right man.'

'Oh yes – and what sort of man would that be exactly?'

'Somebody who'd get me copies of his accounts.'

'And Sheriff Wium – what kind of man would he be after?'

'I'd say he'd be wanting somebody he could be sure wasn't going to tell anybody about his accounts.'

Thorsteinn did not approve of men like Jón Bjarnason; but he rode north again feeling relieved and full of anticipation.

Nothing happened for a week or two; but then the news came up the valley that Sheriff Wium had appointed a deputy. The next time Thorsteinn went over to Hjardarhlíd to ride out with Jens, they were accompanied by the new man – Jón Bjarnason himself. He and Thorsteinn showed no signs of recognition and hardly exchanged a word on the whole journey. But when Jens spoke to him in his usual cutting manner over some point of business, Thorsteinn was now able to look calmly back at him and smile.

But there was to be no quick resolution to his years of waiting. When, after three months, he had received nothing from Jón, he took him aside one day when they were out making the circuit in the district and questioned him.

'Well, I'm sorry, Thorsteinn. I simply haven't had a chance yet.'

'Well, get on and make a chance then. I'm not planning to pay you indefinitely for nothing.'

'Be patient! I'll get you what you want.'

But in fact, when he did finally hand over some copies of the accounts and Thorsteinn checked them with the farmers in question, they proved to be quite correct. He told Jón to try again.

And so it went on, month after month. Sometimes Jón produced nothing; sometimes he produced useless information; occasionally he gave Thorsteinn something which looked promising . . . but never did any of it constitute sufficient evidence for Thorsteinn's ends. There was one day when Thorsteinn lost his patience and threatened to stop paying him; but Jón calmly pointed out that, if this were to happen, he would go straight to Jens and inform him

46

that Thorsteinn had been trying to bribe him. He admitted, with a sly laugh, that it would of course be impossible to prove; but the word would get around all the same . . . And so Thorsteinn curtly handed him his money and rode away across the hill. Jón, smiling to himself, weighed the money in the palm of his hand and then made back for Hjardarhlíd to amuse Jens by telling him that, even after all these months, the old fool Thorsteinn was still paying him in spite of the fact that he had not and never would receive anything. When he heard this, Jens threw back his head and laughed; and, clapping a hand on Jón's shoulder, offered him a drink.

A year or two passed and then in November 1739, while Thorsteinn was over in Breiddalur on business, Jens sent Jón north to hold a preliminary hearing of a case of incest.

3

THE CASE OF SUNNEFA: 1739–43

It was a cold, bright morning in February 1740; and at Bessastadir in Fljótsdalur the large turf-roofed house that stood up on a small rise between the Lagarfljót and the edge of the hills was laden with a thick layer of snow. The winter sun was firing off the banked hills of whiteness and the ice of the frozen lake. A thin wind of steel foraged about the valley, kicking up powder snow on the lower slopes, while out on the high ridges beyond the river it created long, running plumes against the wash of the northern sky. Everything in sight had been quilted over by the heavy snowfall of the past week and the weak twines of smoke that rose from the half-buried farms would have awoken feelings of joyful anticipation in any traveller passing by.

But that morning there were no travellers on the north bank of the Lagarfljót and the only movement, apart from the wild swan passing high overhead, was that of the group of steaming horses that rooted in the snow outside the house at Bessastadir. Now and again, a horse would whinny or snort out a ball of smoky breath: but otherwise the winter silence was edged only by the wind and the flat blade of sound from an unseen stream.

Inside the house, the main room had been cleared and a long trestle table set out along one wall. Behind the table, the handful of men, looking dour and serious, talked among themselves in low voices. In their middle, and yawning in undisguised boredom, sat Jens Wium.

Eventually, a short, black-bearded man, sitting at the end of the bench, leant forward and spoke to him.

'Look, Jens, we made further investigations after the first hearing last November and there seems to be absolutely no doubt about whose child it is. The girl started by naming some Erlendur or other but that seems to have been no more than a ploy. Anyway, this Erlendur wasted no time in denying it and when we asked her again, the girl soon admitted that her brother was the father. Considering their ages, it all seems a bit unlikely – but we'll have to presume that it's the truth. After all, there wouldn't be much point in their lying, would there?'

Jens looked away from the lawyer, Sveinn Sölvason, and turned to his deputy. Jón Bjarnason nodded grimly.

'And what has the boy got to say about it all?' asked Jens.

'Well, he seems bright enough but he just follows whatever his sister says. At that age, you know . . .' replied the deputy. 'As soon as she named him, he admitted it all – he even seemed quite insistent about it when Sveinn here tried to make sure he knew what he was saying. Didn't he?'

The lawyer dipped his head in agreement.

'And do these animals know what the penalty for incest is?' asked Jens.

A white-haired man, a district officer, spoke up.

'Well, sheriff, I told the boy and he seemed to understand all right. But I . . . well . . . I just hadn't the heart to tell the girl – she seemed such a nice child . . .'

'Child!' interrupted Jens. 'And what sort of child is it that sets about seducing her younger brother?' Nobody answered. 'Right – are they both here?'

'They're next door,' said Jón Bjarnason.

Jens made a sign to the man standing by the door and told him to send in the boy. A heavy silence filled the room. Somebody hawked.

The door opened and a tall, lanky youth appeared, stooping to get through the low doorway. He walked slowly out into the middle of the hard, earth floor and stopped in front of Jens.

'Are you Jón Jónsson?'

The boy nodded, swallowing hard.

'Speak up when you're asked a question!' barked Jón Bjarnason.

'Yes, sir,' said the boy.

'How old are you?'

'Fourteen winters . . . I think.' The boy chewed at his lip and looked down. He was exceedingly tall for his age. His still eyes and straight, finely cut nose gave his face a look of sensitivity that combined strangely with his shock of brown hair and his rough clothes. He wore a coarse shirt, heavily patched breeches and something that, in the poor light, resembled shoes. A tattered sheepskin jacket, matted with dirt, reached to the top of his thighs.

'And you have a sister called Sunnefa?'

'Yes, sir, I do,' said the boy, his wide eyes tightening.

'Are you aware of the fact that she gave birth to a boy last October?'

49

'Yes, sir.'

'But, unless I'm mistaken, she's not married. Am I right?' asked Jens with a kind of sweet sarcasm.

'No, sir, she's not married. But she's a good girl and the boy will be cared for,' he blurted out. 'I'll see them right, sir. I'll be a good brother to her.'

'A good brother, eh?' Jens sneered.

'Yes, sir, I will that,' he replied and looked down.

'Boy!' said the sheriff, 'do you know who the father of this child is?'

The boy swallowed and looked round at the roost of faces behind the table. There was not a movement among the six men. He licked his lips and swallowed again.

'Boy, I asked you a question. Do you know who the father of this child is? Answer me.' Jens spoke fiercely.

'Yes, sir, I do, sir,' he said hesitatingly.

'And his name?'

'Well sir . . . it's . . that is . . . it's me, sir.'

The members of the court breathed again and began to murmur to each other.

'But I'll care for the child, sir! And I love her, sir, I do!' the boy cried, twisting his hands together.

In the ensuing silence, Jens spoke with sullen scorn.

'Get out!'

Hanging his head, the boy turned and walked away. As he went, Jens called to the man by the door.

'Send in the girl.'

The boy stopped and turned, his face suddenly older and aggressive.

'Get out!' shouted Jens.

Once the boy had gone, the six men sat waiting in silence. The only noise in the room was that of the sheriff tapping with one finger on the table. Everybody was staring at the door. Apart from Jens, they had all been at the first hearing.

There was something slightly insolent in the manner in which the girl walked in. She came out into the middle of the room, stopped abruptly and stood with her hands behind her back, gently flexing her knees and looking up and down the row of men, almost as if appraising them. She gave a little sniff and rubbed with her finger-tips at the ribs under her breast.

50

She, too, was tall for her age, with a long face, heavy eyebrows and thick, glossy brown hair that fell down her back. She wore nothing but a heavy, woollen shift that reached to the ground and was gathered about her waist with a length of cord. But if it was her lightly built body and her large breasts that first caught the eager looks of the men, it was her eyes that finally held the court in a trance of silence. They were of a rich, dark brown and almost abnormally large, giving her the appearance of being caught in a moment of amazement.

When, finally, somebody coughed and Jens spoke, she gave a little start.

'Are you Sunnefa Jónsdóttir?'

'Yes, sir, I am.' Her voice was soft and low.

'And how old are you?'

'Sixteen winters, sir.'

'Do you have a brother called Jón?'

'Yes, sir.'

'I see . . . And did you or did you not give birth to a boy last October?'

'That I did, sir.'

For a moment, the girl's lips began to tremble.

'And who is the father of this child?' Jens's voice had risen.

The girl looked down at the ground and shifted her feet. When she looked up again, she was frowning as if she were trying to remember. She looked round at the members of the court. For all her seeming confidence when she walked in, she now looked like the mere child she was. The faces before her showed sympathy, fascination, scorn and sorrow.

'And who is the father of the child?'

The girl looked away again.

'Damn it, girl! Will you give me an answer?' Silence. 'Well, then, will you deny that your brother Jón is the father of your child?'

She looked up and turned her shining eyes to Sveinn Sölvason, whom she remembered from the first hearing. Sveinn's face softened into a small smile and he said in a firm but gentle voice:

'Answer Sheriff Wium when he speaks to you.'

It was as if she had been struck over the head. All the tension of her forehead dissolved and her mouth fell open. For a moment she just stared at Sveinn; then the blankness of her face hardened and she turned to Jens with lowered head and compressed lips. She

51

looked like an angry bullock. But Jens, finally losing his patience, brought the flat of his hand violently down on the table and shouted at her to answer him. But even before he had finished speaking, the girl addressed him in a dull, obstinate voice.

'Sheriff Wium.'

'What did you say, girl?'

'Are you Sheriff Wium?' she asked without moving.

'We're not here to talk about my name, damn you! I'm asking you if that young rat of a brother of yours was the person who fathered your child. Answer me!' he bawled.

'Sheriff Wium,' the girl said slowly, 'my mother was Gudbjörg Magnúsdóttir.'

'What in hell's name has your mother to do with it? Now . . .'

'My mother was Gudbjörg Magnúsdóttir at Geitavík in Borgarfjördur.'

There was not a sound in the room. Jens's face had frozen. The girl's eyes held him. But after a moment, he collected himself and said to her in a calm but dark voice:

'I have never heard of her before and I don't want to hear of her now. If you refuse to answer my questions, I shall have to assume that you do not deny that your brother is the father of the child.'

But the girl had not heard what he said.

'My mother, Sheriff Wium, was Gudbjörg Magnúsdóttir at Geitavík in Borgarfjördur.'

'Take the girl away!' cried Jens, his anger flowering once more. He quickly looked down at the table. The piece of paper he held in his hands was bent over double under the pressure of his fingers.

The man by the door stepped forward and took hold of her arm. She shook him off angrily and then screamed at Jens.

'Sheriff Wium, you Danish pig! You remember, don't you?'

Jens did not look up but gestured furiously to the man to get her out of the room. When she had gone, the court broke up into covens of excited whispering while Jens sat staring rigidly down at the table.

The white-haired district officer turned to Sveinn Sölvason.

'What was all that about then?' he said.

'I'm not quite sure,' replied Sveinn. 'Do you know when Thorsteinn Sigurdsson is expected back?'

The district officer shrugged.

'Stupid bitch!' said Jens loudly as he looked up. 'Right then,

52

there's not much doubt about it all, is there? It strikes me that the sooner we get this over the better. If there are no further points you want to raise, we'll get on with pronouncing the sentence. I hereby . . .'

'Jens,' interrupted Sveinn with that gentle voice which his rough looks belied. 'I don't know what sentence you had in mind but don't you think we might consider the circumstances of the case before we go any further. They're nothing but children, you know . . .'

'And since when did children start spawning together like that? Quite apart from the fact that they are brother and sister,' said Jens bitingly.

'Yes, I know. I'm not trying to condone what they've done. But think of their ages – and from what I've learned of their family . . .'

'What the hell has the family got to do with it? We're talking about the boy and the girl who've gone and committed an unnatural act, a crime. Bloody barbaric little animals!'

'I do happen to realize what they've done,' said Sveinn and was about to go on when the old district officer intervened.

'Jens, I agree with Sveinn. With a charge like this which normally carries the heaviest penalty, I think we ought to hear what he's got to say before we take the thing any further.'

'If you'd just let me tell you a bit about their background, I think we might be able to consider a slightly milder sentence than the one you had in mind. May I just do that?' Sveinn asked sarcastically.

Jens shrugged.

'Be brief,' he said, 'I'm wanting to get home.'

'First of all then, may I remind you that however unnatural – as you call it – incest may be, we all know that it's common enough these days. So don't let's get this case out of proportion. Secondly, may I ask you if you really think it's right that a sentence of death should be passed on two people of their age purely because of one mistake they made, no doubt on a cold winter's night when . . .'

'Oh, for God's sake!' exploded Jens. 'Don't start giving us all that soft stuff. They'd probably been at it for months. Next, you'll be giving us some heart-breaking story about them being orphans . . .'

Jens stopped suddenly in mid-sentence. Sveinn looked up at him curiously.

'How did you know they were orphans?' he said slowly. 'It didn't come out at the first hearing.'

'What? I didn't know they were. I was just imagining the kind of thing you were likely to bring up . . .' blustered Jens. 'Look, I've had enough of all this prattling. I'm in charge of this court and I say that they've committed a crime against nature and should be punished accordingly. The child's been born and they both admit to the deed. The law states quite clearly that incest should be punished with death. It's quite simple really, isn't it?' He added this with cloying condescension. Nobody spoke.

'In heaven's name, what more do you want?' he cried.

It was clear that Jens had made up his mind. Sveinn did not wish to waste his energy arguing pointlessly with Jens. But he retorted quickly.

'If it's the death penalty you're asking for, it'll have to go to the Great Assembly this summer, won't it?'

'Of course, of course,' snapped Jens irritably. 'Right, so we're all agreed then. Jón, you can take over and make the formal pronouncement to them. I'm off home.'

He got up and pushed roughly past the men. As he slipped into his heavy, bearskin coat, he turned and spoke to his deputy again.

'Oh yes and Jón – don't forget to get the child adopted quickly. Somewhere up in the north would do well. As for the boy and girl, I think you'd better put them to work on separate farms around here so that we can keep an eye on them. Try old Gísli up at Adalból as a start – he's been short of a man for some months now.'

Before anyone had time to answer, Jens Wium, looking satisfied and comfortable in his heavy coat, nodded to the court and ducked out through a small door in the corner of the room.

'Bastard!' said somebody under his breath. Jón Bjarnason looked round sharply.

Jens rode his tough little Icelandic horse well. He moved quickly away from Bessastadir and followed the indistinct line of the track that led along the Lagarfljót to his home. Every now and again, one of his feet struck against a fat, snow-bound bush of dwarf birch so that a small explosion blew up about him. He passed behind Hjardarhlíd and then came down to the river again at the ford. He made his way over the river and, coming out on the unbroken snow beyond, turned to follow the bank up Nordurdalur below the heights of Múli.

His face was set in thought. He thought first of the court-room and the girl and cursed his luck. Well, perhaps nothing would come of all that, though it was the last thing he needed just at that moment.

54

He thought too of his life at Hjardarhlíd. With Hans away in his first job, as sheriff in the Vestmannaeyjar, and Gudný already of a marriageable age, the prospect of a life alone with that shrew of a wife of his was what worried him most. Something needed to happen . . .

He turned his horse up the steep slope that formed the northern flank of Múli and, cutting diagonally across the hillside, began to climb laboriously through the deep snow. As he gained height, his horse began to move more easily for here the winds had blown the snow off the roundings of the land, leaving patches of the frozen earth almost clear.

He let his horse find its own way uphill and gave himself over to the thoughts that were gathering pace in his mind. As he finally neared the top, he looked up with bright eyes and the outline of a smile on his face and urged on his mount in sudden impatience. The horse came powerfully up the last slope, jerking and stamping its way free amidst showers of snow while the man grinned broadly and gave it little grunts of encouragement.

Up on the top of Múli, Jens sat for a moment looking around. If he still smiled, it was not at the beauty of what he saw but at the thoughts which filled his head. Setting his horse into a slow trot, he moved off across the back of the headland and, having passed a spattering of frozen lakes, came out above Sudurdalur, where the blue smoke of Hvannabrekka could be seen stealing upwards at the head of the valley.

He stayed there for a while, staring down, his eyes narrowed against the cold wind, his mouth puckering from time to time in amusement. Later, he swung his horse round and set off home. Out by the lakes, he halted and, dropping the reins, burst out into guffaws of laughter.

*   *   *

Malcolm MacKay, captain of the *Kittiwake*, out from the Kyle of Tongue in Sutherland, peered through the dim light towards the headland of Berunes. A sharp north-westerly was plucking at the shrouds and pushing rank upon rank of small waves away from the land. He swore softly to himself and turned to say something to one of the crew. The man shrugged. Anyway, the captain thought, it would not be his fault if he had to leave without them. He had told the man (what was he called again? he never could get his mouth round these Icelandic names) that he could take them so long as they were sure to meet him to the east of the headland at dawn.

Malcolm MacKay yawned and went to get something to eat.

The waters of Berufjördur, bounded by high mountains, lay calm and shadowed at that hour of a spring morning. But a little later, the quiet of first light was broken by the sound of hoofs and harness approaching along the foreshore; and soon afterwards, a small group of riders rode up to a farmhouse and dismounted. It was as the sky behind the mountains began to pale that a large, open boat came clear of the shadows, bearing the riders out over the metal waters of the fjord.

Back aboard the *Kittiwake*, Malcolm MacKay saw the boat break away from the land. He nodded slowly and, chewing a piece of dried fish and butter, watched them approaching. When he had made the arrangement with the man earlier that week, he had thought to himself that there was something dishonest about him.

He looked up at the sky. Aye, the weather should hold, he thought to himself as he turned to go below.

*   *   *

The wind was of the kind that obliterates all thought. It was not like an ordinary gale that roars about, buffeting this, tearing at that – this wind, rising the previous evening out of an afternoon of cloud-damped sun and mottled waves, had long since blown up into a violent storm. Now, in the last hour before darkness came, it blew with such a changeless, manic, berserker's power of attack that the people of Heimaey in the Vestmannaeyjar seemed stunned, battered into a stupor by it. It was hopeless to fight against the noise: whatever one tried to do, one's thoughts and whole consciousness were dominated by it.

The wind came in off the sea, ricocheting between Helgafell and the bastion of Heimaklettur at the harbour mouth and then drove ferociously at the houses of the village. It struck at them in seamless bands of strength so that every space and cavity was bursting with it. And indoors, too, everything was swollen with noise and strain: floorboards bulged and shivered like canvas, doors and windows shook, every wooden joint and frame pressed to be free. And now the wind, if anything, seemed to have increased. From time to time, it was as if some great plug had been removed, as if the whole world were suddenly breaking loose, being sucked out into eternity. After twenty-four hours of this, people's heads were filled by a great booming void. They wandered around silently with vacant expressions on their faces or just sat huddled by their meagre fires staring blankly like witless children.

Outside, able-bodied people managed to get about if they had to; but anyone frail or lacking strength, young or old, would have been unwise to chance their luck in the storm. Indeed, on the first evening, one elderly woman had stepped out of her house to get some water and had simply been plucked off the ground and thrown half over a wall. So the people of Heimaey, long accustomed to these winds, remained prudently in their homes and waited for the storm to pass.

Hans Wium had been sitting at his desk in the sheriff's house for some hours, going through his papers. There was nothing of great importance in hand at the time but with the excess of professional pride that comes with a first job, he wanted to leave things in scrupulous order for his successor.

He sat puzzling over one document for a while, his forefinger tugging gently at the corner of his eye. Like his father, he was a large man, well-built with thick brown hair and green eyes, a heavy bottom lip and a prominent, though not gross, nose. His clothes sat well on him and gave him a look of physical satisfaction though there was no particular conceit in his manners.

He frowned, more out of annoyance with the wind's incessant hammering than with any obscurity in what he was reading. But eventually he raised his head and spoke in a rather exaggerated fashion against the noise to the small, bespectacled man who stood writing at the desk in the corner.

'Einar,' he said and his voice had a deep roundness to it. 'Einar, you did make a copy of this business with Gudmundur and the fish barrels, didn't you?'

'Yes, yes,' replied the secretary in a quick, nervous voice. 'I have it here if you'd like to see it.'

But Hans just smiled and waved the offer aside and went back to his reading. Einar Eyjólfsson flustered about with his papers for a while longer before settling down again with his quill and falling back into that age-old, scratching rhythm of the scribe. He had been with the sheriff for two years now, ever since Hans had come to take up the post in the islands. Einar still felt nervous with this young man, physically so much larger than him, who had been schooled at Skálholt and then at university in Copenhagen. Einar himself had learned most of what he knew from old Eyvindur, the minister on Heimaey, and had only left the island twice when he had been to visit his brother in Vík í Mýrdal over on the mainland.

When Einar left the room, Hans breathed out deeply and tidied away the papers on his desk. Then, carrying his lamp, he went and sat himself down by the fire. The wind roared and roared . . . He closed his eyes and suddenly there was nothing but the storm, the glimmer of firelight – and the letter that lay in his pocket.

He had never been that close to his father. And yet, for all this, the news of his father's sudden death had come upon him as a momentous event, forcing him to step back and view things afresh. To a son, a father is always a father, even when he inspires more fear than love; and Hans now felt a confusing mixture of both loss and freedom. But already the image of his father was beginning to set into a memory, and one in which the man was a faceless person, cold, selfish and devious. After all the years of fear, that he had half-mistaken for respect, it came to Hans with sudden clarity that he had merely disliked his father.

Hans opened his eyes and stared into the fire. What was he to make of this last letter of his father's? If it seemed sad to be thinking so badly of his father, it seemed far worse to have doubts about his father's death. Perhaps he was wrong, perhaps it was all exactly what it seemed – a farewell letter to his son from a man who knew that he was about to die. Perhaps . . .

'I simply don't believe it,' he said to his wife as she came into the room.

'What?' replied Gudrún, sitting down beside him.

'The letter. God knows I don't want to think that my father died lying but . . . I mean, do you believe it?'

'What, all that about Thorsteinn Sigurdsson? Hans, I don't know. I only met your father once and I've never even seen Thorsteinn.'

'I know – but however much Thorsteinn hated my father, do you really think he'd actually go so far as to arrange to have him kidnapped? And anyway, why take him all the way to Berufjördur? And what about this story of Thorsteinn's niece being used as a lure? That hardly seems likely. And even if all that part's true, what happened in the boat? And where were they going in an open boat like that? Perhaps there was a struggle and my father went over – but it certainly seems odd to me that when the boat was found, there were just the two dead men in it, both local, and absolutely no trace of either my father or that shifty-looking Jón. God! I never did like him. I could quite easily believe that he was playing a double game with Thorsteinn as the letter says.'

'I just don't know, Hans. Look, we'll wait for this wretched storm to pass and then get away as soon as possible. Once we get to Hjardarhlíd, I'm sure Ingibjörg will be able to tell us more about what happened.'

'My mother? For all my father ever spoke to her, I don't see her being much help in sorting this out.' He sighed. 'God, how this wind goes on! For all we know, we'll still be stuck here in a week's time . . .'

'Hans!' said Gudrún, putting her arms round him.

A year or two younger than Hans, Gudrún was the daughter of a Heimaey merchant. She had an austere kind of beauty, with long fair hair and grey eyes in which there showed the coolness of determination. She did, of course, love Hans; but it was a love that was founded on a desire to nurture him so that he might go forwards – and her with him. Spoilt as a child, she had merely carried on her parents' example of putting her first; so that now, at the age of twenty-four, her concern with herself was entirely unconscious. He, as yet still more of a lover than a husband, was the last person to see either her ambition or the fact that, for all her quiet ways, Gudrún Árnadóttir had him firmly in her grip.

'I was talking to old Snæbjörn this afternoon,' she took up again. 'He says it'll blow itself out in a couple of days. We'll be away by Monday, I promise you, so by midweek we'll be up at Hjardarhlíd. Have you got everything sorted out?'

'Yes. And I've told the district officer what to do until the new man arrives.'

They fell silent; and once again the room lay under the hand of the wind. With the darkness outside and no more than a feeble glow from the fire and the single lamp in the room, there was a feeling of total isolation on this night at the end of the winter. Round about in the village that surrounded the harbour, people pressed together for warmth and security. The smells were of fleece and fish-oil, of pickled puffin and fulmar and guillemot, sweat and dung and the black edge of fear. Earlier than usual, they shucked off their shoes and took to their beds where they lay dumbly waiting for sleep to come. They knew that in time all storms pass . . .

★ ★ ★

Arriving back to take over what had been one's childhood home is a strange experience. The house at Hjardarhlíd seemed smaller than I remembered. But more than its shapes and dimensions, I remembered best its smells – the dusty smell of the fish-oil lamps and tobacco in the main room downstairs; the smell of inks and writing sand in my father's study; the smells of mutton and soured milk and burning fat and soot in the kitchen; and – best of all – the smell of waxed wood in the dark corridor which connected the main room with the kitchen and off which were a couple of box-like rooms where my sister and I had been used to play.

My mother was really our whole existence in those early days, for the children on the farm were a good deal older and so had little time for us. And my father appeared only fleetingly in our lives: he was away for weeks on end and then when he came home he would often shut himself up in his study. We were told that he had work to do; but I remember thinking that it must be strange work for I often heard him talking out loud and making quite a noise when I knew him to be alone.

I have a very clear memory of the first time I saw my father drunk. It was on a summer's night when I was six. There had been a lot of talking and shouting downstairs all evening; and as I could not sleep, I came quietly down and went along the corridor towards the kitchen. I could hear my mother sobbing and my father talking to her in a low, angry voice. Then he shouted something at her and I heard him coming towards the door so I quickly stepped into the shadows of one of the small rooms off the corridor. The door burst open and he came stumbling out, with my mother, still sobbing, clinging to his sleeve. But he threw her off and came reeling down the corridor. I was very frightened and could not understand why he was walking so oddly. When he had gone, I sprang out of hiding and ran to my mother. By now, I had quite forgotten about all the shouting and all I could keep doing was to ask what had happened to my father's legs.

When she had calmed me down and put me back to bed, she explained that my father was not very well at the moment because

60

he had been working too hard; but that I was not to worry as he would get better soon.

'He won't have to have wooden legs, will he?' I asked the face that hung over me in the lamplight.

I think it was only a year or so later that I began to connect my father's odd behaviour with the bottles and flasks that I sometimes caught sight of through the study door. Until then it had puzzled me how he could look perfectly well during most of the day and then, in the evening, turn into his angry, heavy-legged state again. But my perplexity was overshadowed by my fear of him for the alcohol fired up his temper so that the slightest, passing contradiction was enough to set him raging.

All through my childhood, things seemed to have been dominated by his drinking. Inevitably, I suppose, we got used to it; and it was not till later, when I was eighteen and just about to go away to school at Skálholt, that there took place a scene which finally added hatred and scorn to my child's fear of him.

He had gone up to Seydisfjördur with the produce which he had collected from the farmers as revenue. Having sold it to the merchants in Seydisfjördur, he would normally have come straight back; but this time he decided to go on north over the hills to see Brønsted, one of the Danes in Borgarfjördur, who was his drinking companion.

When he finally got back home, he was drunk and quite unapproachable. He was covered in mud and filth and claimed to have lost most of the money. How he had come to lose it or whether he had gambled and drunk it away, we never discovered . . . For the three days following his return, he lived like a wild beast. He had come back with a good supply of Danish brandy and although my mother begged him to change and eat some hot food, he would not listen to her and went and shut himself up in the study. And there he stayed for those three days, ignoring all our attempts to get him to come out. At one moment, he did open the door, thinking us gone, and my mother managed to block it with her foot. But he pushed it shut on her foot and though she cried out in pain, he would not release her. It was at this moment that I sprang forwards, wild with anger at my father. I hurled myself against the door and opened it enough for my mother to withdraw her foot.

When I left for Skálholt, a week or so later, I felt that I had quite suddenly grown up. My father had eventually sobered up and had even made some mumbled excuse for his behaviour; but his drunkenness had only given way once more to that locked-off silence in which he was accustomed to spend most of his time at home. And it was the thought that the sick beast of the days before was lying behind those dead eyes that turned my stomach. I saw that I had finally lost any trust in him that I might still have had.

Three years later, when I had finished at Skálholt, I came home for a month or so before going off again, this time to university in Copenhagen. I stayed there for only a year before coming to the conclusion that I had had enough of academics. I went to the department of the Foreign Office that dealt with Iceland and enquired if there were any sheriff's posts vacant back at home. Two months later, I was sheriff in the Vestmannaeyjar. It was when I had been there nearly two years that my father died, leaving me a request that I should come to Múlasýsla and take over his position. I had scarcely been home in seven years: in spite of the sad circumstances, it really was a homecoming.

Yes, it should have been a triumph – coming back after all those years with my new wife to the family house to take up a new and important job . . . But, in fact, it turned out to be nothing of the kind. Gudrún had been sick on the crossing and the ride over from Reydarfjördur had been wet and miserable, with one of the pack-horses going lame while we were caught in a downpour on the top. And after that, as I said, the actual business of arriving back was quite disconcerting. Coming across the ford, I looked up at the house and shuddered – that was my first reaction. But as soon as Gudrún rode up beside me, I realized that all my fears and bad feeling about the house were connected with the memory of my father – and he was gone. Why should Hjardarhlíd not become a good place again?

The day after our arrival, just as soon as my mother thought that I had had sufficient rest, she started on at me. From the look in her eyes when she walked into the room and from what she had hinted at before, I knew immediately what was going to happen.

'Ah, there you are, Hans,' she said.

'I was just trying to get used to the idea of being back. It's quite strange after all these years.'

My mother smiled and nodded as if she had not really heard me.

'When are you going to do it then?' she asked after a moment's silence.

'What?'

'You know what I mean, Hans . . . Go and see Thorsteinn and lay it before him.'

'Mother, what are you talking about? You know perfectly well that I can't possibly just go and accuse the man of something as serious as this. Not without checking everything first. It'd be most unwise. Imagine what it would do for my reputation if I were proved wrong. He's forty years older than me and I've held the job precisely twenty-four hours. It'd be quite ludicrous.'

'Well, you're not trying to suggest that there's any doubt about it, are you?'

'That he hated my father? No, I . . .'

'That he had your father killed.' My mother's voice was hard.

'We don't know that and I am not going to accuse anybody until we do,' I said vehemently.

'Hans,' said my mother more calmly, 'now, look. We've got a letter from your father stating that for some time he'd known that Jón Bjarnason was being paid by Thorsteinn to try and incriminate Jens. That Jón and Thorsteinn eventually hatched a plan to kidnap your father and take him over the hills to Berufjördur. And that to do this they used Thorsteinn's niece . . .'

'Mother, I know all this but . . .'

'Let me finish!' she cried. 'They used that stupid child to distract your father. And while he was talking to her, he was struck over the head. When he came to, he said he was bound and his horse was being led by Jón. They spent the night in a shieling and the following morning were to go down to Berufjördur. After that we know nothing except that the package containing the letter and some county documents was found on the track in Berufjördur. And that two days later a boat came ashore with a couple of dead men in it. It doesn't take much intelligence to see that your father was being taken somewhere – most probably to be pushed overboard in deep water with a rock round his neck – and that in trying to escape, he drowned.'

My mother looked at me triumphantly.

'Yes,' I said, trying to cover my feelings of exasperation. 'That is certainly what the letter says – nobody is questioning that. But just let me ask you a few questions. Firstly, why was it necessary for Jón to involve Sólrún like that? He knew my father quite well enough to be able to take him unawares. Secondly, even if he did decide to use the girl as he says, why did he think it necessary to take her with them? And anyway, did they actually take her? My father doesn't mention it in the letter. And if they didn't take her, which seems most likely, where in heaven's name is she now? But before all this, can you give me one good reason why Thorsteinn and Jón should've wanted to take him all the way to Berufjördur? You know as well as I do that there are hundreds of places up in the hills where one could safely dispose of a body . . .'

It seemed very clear to me that parts of the story had been fabricated; though why my father should have wanted to do this, I could not imagine. But my mother had no time for my reasoning.

'Hans, you're just being difficult. You're just looking for holes in the story. Of course there are things that are unexplained. Your father had only a few minutes in which to scratch the letter – how could he have possibly said everything?'

'Well, fair enough,' said I grudgingly, seeing my mother's obstinate look, 'but let's just leave it at that, shall we? There's absolutely no way of proving the story one way or another – so if you think I'm going up to Hvannabrekka to start accusing an old man of murdering my father, you're mistaken.'

'But he killed him!' cried my mother. 'Hans, that "old man" up at Hvannabrekka killed your father! Your father, do you understand? What are you going to do about it?'

'I'm not going to do anything because I don't think what you say is true,' I said coolly. 'This is my first important job and if you think I'm going to start it by involving myself in some insane feud, you're wrong.'

'And what sort of son do you think you are?' answered my mother, almost in tears with frustration. 'What sort of spineless child have I raised that will hide from the fact that his father was murdered by a vicious old man who lives just up the valley? How can you call yourself his son?'

'Oh, for heaven's sake! Control yourself!' I shouted back, beginning to lose my own temper.

My mother looked furiously at me for a moment and then stalked out of the room. I wandered over to the study and, closing the door, sat down at the desk. I felt angry and dejected. Women! What a way they had of arguing – it was quite unanswerable. You could not keep them on the straight lines of an argument for more than a few seconds at a time. How could my mother, even considering how she felt, how could she simply ignore the facts of the case and use insult and emotional pressure on me to try and achieve her ends? God almighty, I wished she'd just leave me in peace! God, I could do with a drink . . .

My mind stopped dead in horror. A heated discussion with my mother, a retreat into the study and the need for a drink . . . What macabre irony!

It was there and then that I came to a firm decision about Thorsteinn Sigurdsson and his son Pétur. The twenty years of bad feeling between my father and the people at Hvannabrekka were nothing to do with me. In fact, I resolved to ride up to Hvannabrekka as soon as possible and speak openly to Thorsteinn and his son – not in the fashion my mother urged, but in a new spirit of peace. Yes, any alternative was unthinkable. When Thorsteinn died, Pétur would almost certainly take on the job and the hatred would otherwise continue to rule our lives as it had done those of our fathers . . . I felt the warmth of relief and a new strength at this decision.

*   *   *

Hvannabrekka, Fljótsdalur
May 18th 1740

Dear Ólafur,
You'll no doubt have heard about my father's death by now. But knowing how news can get garbled by the time it reaches Reykjavík, I thought I'd write and let you know the truth about what actually happened. I think my father would've liked you to know as you were one of his oldest friends.

From your visits here, I'm sure you'll remember how my father was forever being antagonized by the other sheriff in this part of the county, Jens Wium. This man had absolutely no regard for anybody, neither my father nor any of the farmers in his charge, whom he quite ruthlessly exploited. What's more, it was clear that he was also misappropriating the taxes, though my father never succeeded in bringing to light any firm proof of this. For twenty years, like the true Christian he was, my father attempted to keep the peace between himself and Sheriff Wium, but was met with only arrogance and drunken abuse. And then, only a month or so ago, late in February, this depraved and callous man played his last and most evil trick on my father.

For some reason, Sheriff Wium decided to disappear. Some people said it was because of money matters; I myself think it may have

65

been to do with this wretched case concerning Sunnefa Jónsdóttir and her brother that you've probably heard about. My father, who wasn't present at her trial, was told by Sveinn Sölvason (do you remember him? he came over when you were last here) that there'd been a strange scene at the trial – something to do with the girl's mother. In any case, not only did Sheriff Wium vanish, but the devil of a man went and took my cousin with him. I can't begin to tell you of the sheer misery and rage I've felt over this – though I think you'll understand if I tell you that she and I were to be married at the end of the summer. The men and I were out on the hills for days looking for her. And then we heard that a letter written by Sheriff Wium had been found at a farmhouse down in Berufjördur; and that later, the two men from the same farm were found dead in their boat just up the coast. Of course, we don't know but we now think that he must've got her away to the coast, him and his deputy, a thoroughly bad man who's also disappeared; and that something happened, some sort of fight, in which she – God rest her soul! – and the others were drowned.

But, Ólafur, that wasn't all. Not content with what he'd done, Sheriff Wium also had the macabre idea of trying to lay the blame for the whole thing at my father's feet. This letter of his claims that my father had had the deputy in his pay all the time; and that he'd used my cousin – his own niece! – as a lure. I've come to the conclusion that Sheriff Wium was not just corrupt but also insane.

You can well imagine our feelings here at Hvannabrekka. An investigation was of course quickly set up but even after some weeks didn't seem to be getting anywhere. And then, just under two weeks ago, my father and I were sitting talking when Sheriff Wium's widow turned up. She'd never been here before but I saw straightaway that she hadn't come to pay a social call. She pushed past me and went up to my father, waving her husband's letter under his nose and saying that she was formally summonsing him to make a public confession of his guilt at this summer's Great Assembly. I began to remonstrate with her, but by now, she was shouting and quite out of control, while my father just stood there, chalk-faced and staring. I eventually got her out of the house but as I closed the door, I heard a noise behind me and rushed back to find my father on the floor, gasping for breath and quite unable to speak. Indeed, he never managed to say another word in the short time before he died. He just kept staring at me with a look of what seemed like anger and *determination. It's not something I shall easily forget.*

In the meantime, I've taken on the post of sheriff and am, at this moment, awaiting official confirmation from the governor.

I look forward to paying my respects to you and your wife the next time I come west. In the meantime, please accept this letter as a humble expression of my thanks for all that you did for my father.

Pétur Thorsteinsson

Pétur addressed the letter, sealed it and, leaning back in his chair, smiled sourly. A thin drizzle started to fall and was rushed against the window by the passing breeze. Little by little, the light in the room was beginning to fail.

*   *   *

The pool in the river was deep, its surface steel-flat, with low, dark cliffs hanging over it. Elsewhere, the sky was a broad seamlessness of pale light. A group of men were climbing towards the pool. With them was a woman in a tattered shift, her hands tied, her head hanging.

At the pool, a man gave the sign. Her cries became screams: they were sitting her down, roping her wrists to her ankles. The sack was placed over her; she was twisting and bucking. The sack's mouth had been secured, the men fallen back. Now she was still.

Once more, the sign. She was carried down and then suddenly she was falling, falling forever, and cold darkness was everywhere and no air, no air . . .

*   *   *

Sunnefa woke with a start and lay staring up at the sky with her heart striking heavily. Then she sat up and, wrapping her arms round her knees, buried her face in her skirt and let the tears come.

As a child, she had overheard somebody talking about a woman's execution in the Drowning Pool at Thingvellir. And in the weeks since the trial, she had not been able to free herself from the thought of it. To a girl of her age, the idea of actually being dead was perhaps no more than a remote inevitability. But the image of the sealed sack and the cold, silent water was clear and unbearable.

When at last she had cried herself out, she lay back and watched the pack of clouds passing over the May sky. She felt safe and at ease high on the hill, far from the farmhouse kitchen and yard where everyone seemed set on excluding her. To begin with, she had thought they treated her like that simply because of what she had done; but later she realized that it was the death sentence passed on her that made them so full of circumspection and ill-concealed fascination. The older people were kind enough, though she would sometimes catch them staring at her in the kitchen half-light. But it was the younger ones, with their whispering and covered glances, who made her feel so totally alone.

Ever since she had grown into womanhood, Sunnefa had lived on the edge of unease. By the time she was fourteen, her body had made her seem several years older – and it was this and her simple, open way of behaving that had quickly made her the object of intense interest among the men of the district. Puzzled yet excited, she would let a man near her, perhaps even lead him on a bit before running off, flushed and laughing.

Orphaned at the age of eight, Sunnefa may have lacked someone to warn and to guide her; but by the time she began to attract so much attention, there was already somebody to keep an eye on her. Although a couple of years younger than his sister, Jón was already tall and quite remarkably strong. The two of them, feeling themselves outsiders on the farms where they'd been sent, always kept themselves apart and together. It was largely because of this, their growing up in the closeness of seclusion, that made Jón so resentful when men began to take an interest in his sister. Maybe he sensed that there could be danger in it for her; maybe it was just the simple pique of jealousy – but when she laughed at him, pretending not to know what he meant, he went away determined that if he could not stop her, he would at least make sure that he was on guard for her. In secret, he made himself a short, heavy club, which he took to wearing inside his jacket at all times.

One afternoon, early in summer, Jón was returning to the farm when he saw Sunnefa talking to a man on horseback on the track below. He watched them for a while and saw them turn and go up a small valley. Cutting across the hillside, he eventually found them, far up the valley, sitting by a stream. He crouched down among the rocks and waited. It was later, when he saw the man suddenly take hold of Sunnefa and push her down that he came loping silently from the rocks and brought his club fiercely down on the man's head. Together, he and Sunnefa dragged the man to his horse and, tying him on, set the animal off down the valley. Then, still dazed and scared, they walked away up into the hills, to a place they knew where there was only sunlight and open sky. And it was there, hiding a while from the rest of the world, that they made a new bond between them.

For some time after this, neither of them made any reference to what had taken place that afternoon. For when they heard that the man had been found dead, the fear of it all made them silent and wary. But some of the women of the surrounding farms, sharp-eyed in their jealousy of Sunnefa, noticed that she had changed, that she would no longer have much to do with the men who hung around her.

Time passed: and it was in the dog-days of that summer, when the nights were filled with soft, luminous light and the waters of the sea stretched across the narrow fjord as sleek and heavy as quicksilver – it was in these days that she went with her brother again. One evening as they all sat outside the farm, she turned to Jón.

'Let's go for a walk, shall we? Not now,' she whispered. 'Later . . .'

Down on the shore by the turf hut where the men from the farm kept their fishing tackle, down by that weighted, sleeping water while the whole world lay suspended in warmth and stillness, the boy and the girl met. Their dusty, summer flesh dry and floury beneath their hands; and their words mixing with the whistling flight of duck and the calling of lambs.

It is perhaps the second meeting of lovers that seals their pact; and from that summer night onwards, the bond between Sunnefa and Jón grew swiftly stronger. Most of the others merely laughed at them for their loyalty to each other; but, by and large, people let them be, most of them only too thankful that the girl was no longer the troublemaker she had been over the previous winter.

And so the summer months passed for them in the strange blending of happiness and pain that would seem to be at the heart of love. But then summer became autumn, and slowly the shortening of the days gave them less and less chance of being alone. It was as autumn moved into winter, in that darkest corner of the year, that a change came about.

There was a man called Erlendur Erlendsson who had settled round the headland in Njardvík. He was a wealthy man, tall with a slight stoop and thin legs. He had lost two fingers of one hand as the result of a drunken wager at a celebration following the birth of his daughter. As his wife had just died and as his daughter was still a mere child, he arrived in Njardvík on the look-out for a woman. He happened to call in at the farm and was immediately taken by the silent girl who was sent to serve him a bowl of broth. A week later he returned and made an offer for the girl. The farmer told Erlendur that he would speak to the girl and promised him a definite answer by Easter. Erlendur went away home feeling confident.

When Sunnefa was told about this, she refused even to consider it and asked the farmer both to put aside the idea and to make no mention of it to Jón. The farmer, secretly relieved, agreed to let the matter rest. So he was somewhat surprised when, a month or so later, Sunnefa came to him and asked if she might borrow a horse, explaining that she wanted to ride over to Njardvík to see Erlendur. Jón, who knew nothing of this until she had gone, would not leave her alone on her return. Finally, she turned on him in exasperation.

'Well, I'll tell you then! I've been over to see Erlendur Erlendsson in Njardvík.'

'What on earth do you want with him?' asked Jón.

'Who said I wanted anything with him?'

'Then why did you go, for God's sake?'

'Because he wants something of me, that's why. He wants me to be his wife.'

'I'll tear him apart if he comes anywhere near you again,' said Jón slowly.

'Listen, Jón! I'm pregnant. When the baby's born, I'm going to have to name a father. So I had to go, I had to let it be seen I was going to him.'

One day just before midsummer, Sunnefa was down at the stream rinsing out some clothes. The old woman next to her suddenly spoke.

'Have you made up your mind what you're going to say then?'

'About what?' replied Sunnefa innocently.

The old woman paused and looked round at the shape of her belly, which Sunnefa had long since given up trying to hide.

'You'll have to name the father, you know. Gudbrandur, the minister, will need to know for the church records. So what'll you say?'

'Well, the truth, I suppose.'

'Yes,' said the old woman thoughtfully. 'Yes, that's always meant to be the right thing to do, isn't it? But don't you think that there might be times when it's better to tell a . . . that is, to say something other than the truth? I mean, when it's a question of saving your skin . . .'

'It all depends, doesn't it?' interrupted Sunnefa. 'As far as I'm concerned, I can't see any reason why Erlendur shouldn't accept the responsibility when I name him.'

'No – except of course if he decides that the child isn't his.'

Sunnefa lowered her head and beat angrily at the clothes.

'Look, child,' said the old woman, putting her hand on the girl's arm. 'Be sensible. If Erlendur wants you, will you have him?'

'No!' said Sunnefa darkly.

'Not even if that's the only way of saving you both?'

Sunnefa shook her head vigorously.

'So why should the man accept your naming of him as father then?'

The girl shrugged, her face now heavy with misery.

'You know as well as I do,' went on the old woman, 'that there are some round here who wouldn't be sorry to see you in trouble. And if Erlendur rejects your naming of him and if these people choose to speak up, then you two are done for . . . Listen, I tell you what – name Erlendur and if he refuses to accept it, then I'll bear witness that I saw him with you that day when he accompanied you back from Njardvík. He's a wealthy enough man: he can afford to look after another child.'

By the time autumn arrived and Sunnefa was within a few weeks of giving birth, the word went round that the old woman knew something which would protect the girl. There were indeed people who wished Sunnefa harm – but was the feeling against her so strong that things might actually have been arranged to block her help? This was never to become clear: but shortly before the child was due, the old woman had a bad fall while over at a neighbouring farm and was unable to travel home until it was too late.

In the last hours of an October night, Sunnefa gave birth to a boy. The following day, the minister appeared and asked the girl who the father was. Sunnefa named Erlendur. Erlendur, when informed of this, sprang on to his horse and rode over to see the girl. Nobody knew whether the colour of his face was due to anger or anticipation. He spoke to Sunnefa in private for a few minutes and when he left, he went straight to Gudbrandur the minister and made it quite clear that he denied any responsibility for the child. At that, the minister told Sunnefa that he would stay until she gave him a name. Weak and now frightened, she began to call out for her brother: but he was carefully being kept away from her at the other end of the building. In the end, as this was the only name she would say, it was deemed sufficient evidence of her guilt; and Gudbrandur, a self-righteous man who had formerly cast his eyes at her, sent off the necessary letter to the sheriff. Word came back that the boy and the girl were to be held separately, pending the court of enquiry that was to be convened a week later . . .

Sunnefa blinked and sat up. If she could only see Jón! In the five months since the meeting of the court at Bessastadir, she had had no news of him and now did not even know where he was being held.

For a long time after the trial, she had been half-mad, with scarcely a thought for Jón or their sentence. To begin with, they had told her that her son was to stay with the wet-nurse until the trial was over; only later did she discover that in fact the child had long since been given to foster-parents far away in the north. When she screamed at them, begging to have her child back, they told her that in the end it would be better for him this way. Later, she fell into a state of silence and apathy, with sudden fits of tears and a violent anger against herself.

She got to her feet, shook her hair back from her face and looked down into the valley. Across the wet, sleeping eel of the Lagarfljót, she could make out the house at Hjardarhlíd. She wondered what truth there had been in the stories she had heard about the disappearance of Sheriff Wium so soon after the trial. She must ask Kristín if anything further had been discovered – Kristín, who had a squint and whose ankles were not right, was virtually the only person who would talk to Sunnefa. She was another outsider.

*   *   *

It was all hot and smoky in the house so I got out as fast as I could after the meal. I suppose you can't very well hope to get some decent hot food without a fire, can you? But all the same I let the woman know what I thought of her wretched smoking fire. She's one of the ones who's had it in for me right from the beginning. So when I started complaining she soon told me to shut up. But by then I'd got my bowl full and had nothing to lose – so I gave her a piece of my mind. Christ, you should've seen the way the old hag reacted! Not a word, not a sign that she'd even heard what I'd said, but just as I was looking down to drink some soup, she spun round and caught me one across the head with the big wooden ladle. Everyone had a good laugh at that. I swore at her again and must've really touched her on the raw this time for her face went all mean like. 'Hey, Jón lad, you'd better learn to mind your tongue,' she said. 'I'd hate to fetch you too good a one across the neck and rob the headsman of his fun next month at Thingvellir.' There was a sudden silence in the room at this quip of hers but I just laughed. 'I won't be hob-nobbing with the headsman at Thingvellir this year, you old sow,' I replied. 'In fact, there's not a chance that you'll keep out of the grave long enough to see me go that way at all. And make sure you give us better food than this swill in future. Or you're going to find yourself on the way to Thingvellir – on a charge of man-slaughter.'

But once away from them all, my mood changes completely. I can carry on all that brave stuff when I'm with them; in fact, I've got to, because if they ever knew how I really feel – well, I'd get no peace at all from them. To tell the truth, I almost bite through my tongue when I think of the headsman. But I could face it all if I just had some news of Sunnefa. If only I could see her! Nobody understands her as I do. And as for thinking of what they'll do to her if it goes against us at Thingvellir . . . O Sunnefa, my beautiful Sunnefa! I won't let them, I promise!

*   *   *

Well, Kristín, it was like this . . . There I was, on my way back from the hill and strangely enough I'd just been thinking how I wanted to ask you about Sheriff Wium's disappearance. Well any-way, as I was saying, there I was, walking along the track when I saw these two horsemen riding towards me. I wasn't too keen on coming up with a couple of men by myself – but, first of all, they'd already seen me and, secondly, I could tell by the way the sun glinted on their harness that they were no ordinary men. So I walked on, trying to look as unconcerned as I could and hoping that they'd ride straight past me. Anyway, I was out of luck because when they were a short way off, they slowed their horses to a walk and stopped talking. I could feel them staring at me. But I kept my eyes on the ground and had almost got past them when one of them called out.

'Hey, girl!'

The man who'd spoken to me was large, well-built . . . I'd say quite nice-looking on the whole. I had the feeling that I'd seen him somewhere before. I suppose I must've been staring at him and trying to work this out because I didn't really take in what the other man said when he spoke to me.

'I'm sorry, sir – what did you say?'

'I asked you where you were going.'

'Me, sir? I'm just on my way back to the farm. Up there.'

Oh, Kristín, this other man was quite different. I suppose some people would say that he was good-looking. Well, perhaps he was, but in such an ugly, such a bad sort of way. He had this heavy white forehead and dark sunken eyes that made you want to shiver. And he was a big, strong brute too – the same sort of build as the other man but the strength made this one look lumpish and nasty. Both of them were well dressed and had fine horses with brass harness. And I kept noticing the big silver ring the first man wore. Anyway, I turned away from the dark man. I couldn't bear his gaze – it was as if he were looking right through me. But then the other one spoke to me again.

'Well, girl, what's your name?'

'Her name's Sunnefa Jónsdóttir,' said his companion before I had time to answer.

The first man frowned and looked intently at me.

'Is that so? So you're Sunnefa, are you?'

'Yes, sir. That's me, right enough.' For a moment I felt quite pleased that these two men should know of me; but then, of course, I realized that it would only be because of the trial. I started to walk off but the first man laughed and called out to me.

'Hey, Sunnefa! Come back here a moment. Come on, don't be afraid.'

I walked slowly back. He looked down at me, smiling; and then, with a soft laugh, turned to his companion.

'By God, she's just as beautiful as they say, isn't she? Don't you think so?'

The dark man, facing me across the neck of the other man's horse, didn't smile. He just stared at me with those eyes of his and his tight lips.

'Yes,' he said finally but without changing his expression.

74

'Here now, Sunnefa,' said the other man in a warm sort of way. 'Are they treating you all right on the farm? Don't be frightened to say if they're not. How did you go and get yourself into this scrape, child? Things aren't going to be easy for you.'

I didn't answer. What was there to say?

'Well, we'll be seeing you again soon.'

He started to turn his horse away but halted because the other man, beyond him, was sitting staring at me. Oh, Kristín, I tell you, I don't like that man, he really frightens me . . . Well, after a moment, he gave me a curt nod and off the two of them rode, all jangling and shining like. But the silly thing is, Kristín, I never really worked out who they were exactly . . .

And Kristín had wrinkled up her nose and told her what a silly goose she was. Didn't she realize that she'd been talking to the two sheriffs – the dark one, Pétur Thorsteinsson of Hvannabrekka, and the other, Hans Wium from Hjardarhlíd? She'd best be civil to them – they were the most important people in her life just at that moment.

'Wium? I didn't know that the old sheriff had a son. Is he married?'

'Who? Hans Wium? Yes, he's married.'

'What's she like?'

'Oh, she's good-looking. In a hard sort of way. They say her husband's devoted to her.'

*   *   *

It was dusk, that floating, formless dusklight which merely joins one afternoon to the following morning during the summer months of the north. The stillness in the big room at Hvannabrekka was total and gave the man the look of a corpse as he sat motionless at the desk, staring into the dimness in front of him.

It was well into the night. Gunnlaug, Pétur's foster-mother, had long gone to bed; and all the people who helped work the farm were asleep in the loft. Pétur Thorsteinsson was, as usual, quite alone.

The room, though big by average standards, was not in fact very large. The floor and ceiling were of wood; and the walls, though of stone and rubble, were also lined with planks – so that the general impression was one of a simple wooden box, unrelieved other than by the two small, square windows and the door. This bareness might have been offset by pictures or wall-hangings, by rugs or curtains or pots or other trinkets; but in fact there was little sign of such things. The furniture consisted of the small wooden desk, long past its prime, and its chair; and two other wooden chairs placed about a tattered horseskin rug. In the far corner of the room stood a large traveller's chest, while on the wall above the desk, a single shelf carried a Bible and two books on Danish law.

Eventually, Pétur reached out and took a drink from the glass of water on the desk. He then helped himself to a few spoonfuls of the curds which Gunnlaug had left him but pushed the bowl away without finishing it. He sat back for a moment and then, lighting the little fish-oil lamp, unlocked a drawer in the desk and took out a thin, flat book. As he prepared his quill, there was a sour look on his face. He opened the book, dipped the goose feather into the ink and wrote.

June 12th 1740

Rode out with HW today. He wants my friendship. Let him want. I must bide my time and not be overhasty.

We met the girl Sunnefa out by the Lagarfljót. HW seemed to take a fancy to her. Is there a way in this? I don't know . . . But I shall let the Good Lord, Our Blessed Saviour Jesus Christ, guide me in this as in all things.

He wiped the excess of ink off the quill and, staring down at what he had written, picked up the spoon and finished the curds. When this was done, he reached up to the shelf and took down the Bible. Sitting bolt upright at the desk with the first two fingers of one hand resting against his temple, he sat and read selected passages from the book for half an hour or so. Then he replaced it on the shelf, locked up his journal and, picking up the lamp, went to bed.

*   *   *

The Great Assembly at Thingvellir, the country's annual legislative and judicial gathering, was to start, as in previous years, on July 8th. In order to be there in time, people riding over from the east had to set out nearly two weeks in advance. Thus it was proposed that the party taking Sunnefa and Jón should leave at the end of the third week in June.

But early in that month, Sunnefa fell ill. She complained of stomach pains and headaches, and soon was unable to hold down any food. They taunted her, saying that she was doing this on purpose so that she would be unable to make the journey west; but she just shrugged at this and turned her face to the wall. They called in the doctor, Björn, but he could find nothing wrong with her. But by the time they were due to leave for Thingvellir, he said that it was quite out of the question for her to travel as she was now so weak.

When the doctor's report was brought round to Hjardarhlíð, Gudrún had been trying to persuade her husband to use the opportunity of going on from Thingvellir to Reykjavík so that he could go and make himself known to the governor, Joakim Lafrentz.

'But whatever for?' laughed Hans.

'Well, I can't see there's any harm in passing by and introducing yourself.'

'Passing by! Gudrún, the governor's house is not exactly on the way between here and Thingvellir, you know. And anyway, why should he care to see me, a young sheriff from the other side of the country?'

'How do you think people get from being young sheriffs to men of importance? So you're riding in to Reykjavík to get me one or two little things and while you're there you happen to remember Joakim Lafrentz's liking for French wine. So you take him a case.'

Hans threw back his head and laughed.

'What a wife I've got myself!'

'I only want the best for you, Hans. I don't like to see you hiding your light under a bushel. I'll not stand by and see you waste your talents.'

'But, Gudrún, a whole case! You know that we don't normally see more than a bottle or two of it from one year to the next.'

'Don't make so much of it, Hans. And anyway, while you're there, you can always buy me something nice too,' she said with a smile.

When the doctor's note arrived, Hans sat down heavily in the morning sunshine, his former good spirits now dissipated.

'Well, that's a shame. That's a great shame,' he said after a few moments. 'I'd been counting on getting this business cleared up as soon as possible. My father's sentence was far too harsh. I'm sure the Assembly would've seen fit to put in a plea for clemency. And now the wretched children will have to wait a whole year for their sentence to be reviewed.'

He sighed and fell silent.

'Look,' he said, 'with them being so young, I think it'd be best to get them where I can keep an eye on them. I'll send one up to Pétur at Hvannabrekka and we'll have the other here. I don't think Hvannabrekka's much of a place for a young girl. No, I'll send him the boy. If we have the girl here, I'm sure Gudný will keep an eye on her.'

'Fine,' said Gudrún slowly. 'I'll be interested to see this girl. I've heard so much about her. Is she really that beautiful?'

'Yes . . . well, I suppose you could say so. You couldn't call her plain, certainly. But I hadn't really noticed, to tell the truth.'

Gudrún smiled to herself.

When his wife had gone indoors, Hans fetched his horse and rode over to Hvannabrekka.

*　　*　　*

June 24th 1740

HW came over today to ask me to take the boy J in as there can be no hearing at the Great Assembly this year owing to the girl's sickness.

My father told me two things about the trial at Bessastadir that he had heard from Sveinn Sölvason. 1. That whatever it was that the girl S knew about JW, it inspired a great hatred in her. 2. That the boy J, her brother, was very much in his sister's power.

So – I have J: J loves S: S hated JW (and therefore HW?): S is in HW's house. Can this chain be made to work? Two questions. 1. Did S know who HW was when we met on the road the other day? She showed no animosity to him. 2. Can I discover from J (if he knows) what it was that made S hate JW so much?

*　　*　　*

Nearly a month later. The Great Assembly at Thingvellir has closed and men are once again crossing the country on their way home. For two days the whole of Múlasýsla has been swept by a series of violent rainstorms which have turned the rough tracks along the banks of the Lagarfljót into bands of heavy mud. The surrounding hills are buried in cloud and thick veils of rain.

Going west along the south bank of the Lagarfljót, Sunnefa, looking pale and drawn from her recent illness, rides her horse in the fashion of the poor women, sitting astride the animal with her knees drawn up higher than its back. Her hunched posture reflects everything she feels. She is accompanied by an old man who has been told to take her to Hjardarhlíd. The rain pours down, spikes the surface of the water beside them, kicks up the mud in the pools, turns the two of them into dark, sodden bundles.

As they reach the end of the Lagarfljót and turn towards the ford, two horsemen pass across them heading south towards Sudurdalur. About fifty yards separate the two parties in the driving rain. One of the horsemen looks round. Reining in his mount, he pulls up his companion to whom he is tied.

'Hey! Sunnefa!' he shouts.

The girl starts up in amazement.

'Jón!'

But the old man takes the reins of her horse and leads her off at a fast trot towards the ford. By the time they reach the house at Hjardarhlíd, she has stopped crying. The rain still pours down.

*   *   *

On the whole, Hans Wium had been right in saying that life at Hvannabrekka would have been grim for a young girl. There was no doubt that the hillside looming up behind the buildings contributed to this spirit of melancholy; but there was equally little doubt – especially in the mind of Jón – that the people at the farm were also a cause of this oppressiveness.

Of the people working at Hvannabrekka, there were half a dozen who actually lived on the farm. Apart from Gunnlaug, who spent most of her time in the main house, there were two other women – one decrepit old creature well into her eighties and a girl in her late teens, swarthy-faced and bullish. The menfolk consisted of two unmarried brothers in their fifties and a younger man, Gudjón. He was gross and had blue pig-eyes and a small effeminate mouth.

One evening late in August, they were all sitting in the kitchen eating their supper. Gunnlaug had forgotten to trim the lamp and the light was smoky and bad. Jón, still hungry after a meagre meal, picked up a piece of bannock from the table and ate it.

'Hey, you greedy runt!' said Gudjón. 'That was mine. Don't you ever do that again or I'll give you a dusting.'

Jón, long aggravated by Gudjón's manner, flared up.

'Shut your face, lard-guts! You couldn't give a dusting to a half-dead chicken!'

The brothers nudged each other.

'Mind yourself, lad,' said one of them. 'Our Gudjón here fancies himself at the wrestling.'

'Pah!' retorted Jón. 'You don't think he scares me, do you?'

'Right,' said Gudjón. 'I think it's time we showed this shoddy little sister-lover a lesson, don't you, boys?'

Jón sprang to his feet. The girl's eyes narrowed and the two brothers grinned in anticipation.

'For God's sake leave him alone, can't you, Gudjón,' said Gunnlaug. 'You ought to be ashamed of yourself – he's not even half your age.'

'Shove off, woman!' said the man sharply. 'This is men's business here. It's about time the cocky brat was taught a lesson.'

Afterwards, when the moon had risen, they went outside. The two brothers lit their pipes and sat side by side against the wall of the house, while the girl stood in the doorway biting her thumb.

Gudjón, whose temper had cooled and who was now mainly intent on showing off, asked Jón if he had ever done this Icelandic wrestling before.

'No, but I'll learn faster than you think. Let's get on with it.'

They stripped to the waist and padded out on to the flat grass. Then they began to circle each other, half-crouched, the moon throwing a cold, waxen light on their flesh.

'Come on,' whispered Gudjón provokingly. 'Don't be afraid – I won't hurt you that much.'

He had hardly spoken when the boy's right arm flashed in the cool light. Gudjón recoiled under the impact and his arms beat at the hand holding tight about his throat. Jón stood firm, legs braced, his other arm behind his back, everything concentrated along his forearm into the power of grip for which he had been so well-known in Borgarfjördur. There was a sternness in his face, strange for his age, as he held the man till at last Gudjón's arms dropped.

Jón turned away and began to put on his shirt.

'Well, lad, that's not exactly the way we wrestle,' said one of the brothers, 'but, by Christ, you put him down well. Here, let's have a feel of your hand . . . God Almighty, you could bend iron! How old are you?'

'What's that got to do with it?' said Jón, pushing past him into the house.

Now Jón was completely alone. And so summer passed and the autumn began.

*　　*　　*

Hans's sister, Gudný, now eighteen, was only a year older than Sunnefa. She was on the tall side, a personable sort of girl whose attractiveness was as much due to her bright and lively character as to her looks. All through their childhood, she had looked to Hans for support and alliance amidst all the anger and recriminations of their parents. With Ingibjörg ever more more sharp and difficult since Jens's death, it was a joy for Gudný to see Hans come home. It was an easy extension of her love for him that soon made her fast friends with his wife.

By the end of that first summer after Jens's death, when Sunnefa Jónsdóttir came to live at Hjardarhlíd, Gudný saw that Gudrún had misgivings about having this dark-eyed girl on the farm. Intent on making the best of an uneasy situation, Gudný decided to go out of her way to befriend Sunnefa, hoping by this to draw her in rather than keep her on the outside of the household, from where she could be more of a problem. But Sunnefa, having initially warmed to Gudný's kindness, only later discovered who she was and immediately became no more than coldly deferential when the older girl came to talk to her.

'Don't waste your time on her,' said Ingibjörg one day on hearing Gudný and Gudrún talking of Sunnefa. 'In my opinion, it would've been better if they'd done away with her on the spot as Jens suggested.'

'How can you say that?' cried Gudný. 'You wouldn't say that if she were your daughter.'

'Well, she's not my daughter. And I do say it,' replied her mother intransigently.

'Why do you think she's so unwilling to talk to you?' asked Gudrún.

'I don't know. It was strange – she was quite friendly until she realized who I was. I explained that I wished her no ill, that Hans wanted to help her . . .'

'When did he say that?' interrupted Ingibjörg sharply. 'Why

doesn't Hans learn where to use his energies? My God, he won't do anything to advance himself, yet he goes and decides to help an unnatural brat who's already shown herself to be a thankless good-for-nothing.'

'That's just not true! She's never been given a chance. Father didn't give her much consideration from what I've heard.'

'From what you've heard!' said Ingibjörg, turning on her daughter. 'And what have you heard, may I ask? Just idle gossip among the girls, I'll be bound. Well, I'll tell you the truth. Your father – God rest his soul – would have been generous enough with her if he'd had the chance. But no, the little bitch just shouted at him and called him "a Danish pig".'

'Who called whom "a Danish pig"?' asked Hans, coming into the room behind his mother. He suspected that she was on about Thorsteinn Sigurdsson once again. Hans had not forgiven his mother for her visit to Hvannabrekka that day and was determined to stamp out any further references to the old feud.

'Who called whom "a Danish pig", mother?' he asked again.

'Oh nobody, Hans . . . I was just telling a silly story I'd heard.'

But Gudný could not stop thinking about the story and eventually forced herself to ask Sunnefa if it was true.

'I never said that,' Sunnefa replied to Gudný's question. 'What would I have had against your father. He was just doing his work. Who told you that?'

'Oh, my mother said she'd heard it somewhere . . . She must've been mistaken.'

'Yes, she must,' said Sunnefa.

As Gudný closed the door behind her, Sunnefa spat.

'God rot his soul,' she said with feeling.

*　　*　　*

There was a man called Jóhann Thorvardsson. He was a young farmer who lived at Tó just up the valley. He was the best man in the district with the horses and was often asked to go and give advice by the other farmers when they had problems with their animals. The other thing he was interested in was women. He was often over at Hjardarhlíd that summer.

He was a big, weather-beaten man of thirty-five, who always wore a flamboyant neckerchief and whose broad smile and dark eyes had, it was reputed, been the undoing of women of all ages throughout the district. It was tacitly agreed that no woman could consider herself full-fledged unless Jóhann from Tó had made a set at her.

When Jóhann from Tó first set eyes on Sunnefa, he was busy attempting to seduce a rather prim girl who had been at Hjardarhlíd for the summer months. Jóhann had seen this girl's prudery as a challenge; but by the end of the summer he had not achieved very much and was beginning to find her virtue rather tedious. And so when, one day in August, he raised his head from whispering sweet nothings into the girl's ear and happened to see Sunnefa walking across to the farm, the change was dramatic. He said 'See you later' and the girl replied 'What?' and he had gone.

Sunnefa was not interested and yet was also not displeased. She listened to his honeyed words, smiled and walked away. A day or two later, Jóhann was back, too experienced to be seriously in danger of losing his heart yet all the same already obsessed by the girl.

All through that month of September, the game continued. Watching at the farmhouse window, Hans felt his sense of duty confused by a growing excitement. He kept telling himself that he would speak to Jóhann: the girl, after all, was his ward. Yet for all he said this, the days continued to pass without anything being done.

Before the autumn, Hans was due to ride out with Pétur to oversee the collection of the taxes. Each farmer was liable for an annual land-tax which was usually paid to the sheriff in dried fish, tallow, fox-skins, wool and woollen goods. Over and above this, there was a rent for the permanent stock of beasts on the farm which was traditionally paid in butter. Once the sheriff had collected these dues, it was his responsibility to sell the goods to the Danish merchants, who were part of a monopoly company with a charter from Copenhagen. Of the money he received from this sale, the law allowed the sheriff to keep one third in the form of his salary while the rest had to be handed over to the king's steward in the west.

Although this should have been a time of hope and optimism, Hans set off sullen and depressed. He and Pétur did their rounds quickly, sold the goods to the first merchant they met in the fjords and then leaving Pétur to some further business, Hans turned for home and rode swiftly back to Hjardarhlíd.

As soon as he got back, he went to look for Sunnefa. He found her out behind the farm, milking a cow.

'I want to talk to you,' he said brusquely.

'Yes, sir,' she said without looking up.

'Has that Jóhann been bothering you again?'

'Jóhann, sir?'

'Yes. You know who I mean – Jóhann from Tó.'

'Has he been bothering me, sir?' asked Sunnefa archly, looking up at Hans.

'Yes . . . well . . . that is – I've noticed that he's been coming over to see you quite often this past month.'

'Well, sir, it's true he's spoken to me on occasions. But nothing special like. He speaks to everyone, sir. I don't really know what you mean.'

'It's just that I'd gathered that he was always pestering you.'

'Me, sir? Who told you that?'

'Nobody told me. I . . . Oh, it doesn't matter,' he said angrily.

'No, sir.'

She watched him as he strode off.

The very next day, Jóhann was back at Hjardarhlíd again.

★   ★   ★

The hooped moon, brilliant and full, broke clear of the towering castles of cloud that drove across the sky. The wind, strong and sharp, flattened the milky grasses and tossed about flurries of spray from the mountain waterfalls. Down at the farm, it made soft, soothing noises as it slid over the roofs of the houses.

Gudrún shifted in her sleep and then suddenly was awake. She lay there with her eyes still closed, sensing her husband's breathing beside her.

'Can't you sleep?'

'No.' His answer had an angry exhaustion to it.

'What's wrong?'

'Nothing.'

'Tell me, Hans. Please.' She turned towards him. 'There's been something on your mind for weeks now.'

'No, really, it's nothing,' he said, putting his arm round her. 'It's just that I don't seem to be able to sleep too well these days, that's all.'

Gudrún shut her eyes in weariness.

★   ★   ★

Throughout the autumn, the tenuous balance of this situation was somehow maintained. But as the days got shorter and the weather rougher, longer hours were spent in the confines of the small buildings, and tempers began to be strained.

And then, just after Christmas, when everyone felt that, with the turning of the year, the distant spring was slowly coming nearer, it began to snow. It came in the dark on the back of a stiff north-easterly, one evening just as they were sitting down to a meal of mountain-moss soup. All through the night it continued to drive in over the farm so that by first light the next day they found themselves completely snowed in, doors, windows blocked over; and, out beyond, a world of smoking white chaos as the gale-force wind streamed in.

For six days and nights the blizzard blew on unbroken. And then as the wind finally dropped and the clouds passed away over the hills, the temperature began to fall. By evening, with the stars masked by the swirling columns of the northern lights, the frost's grip was tightening hard: milk freezing, fish-oil thickening, flesh gluing to metal, doors suddenly rigid at hinge and jamb.

In the morning, they tugged at the door, grinding away the ice, and stepped out into the chilled pit that was the remains of their path to the byre. Shovels clattered on the walls of ice as the men clawed their way upwards towards the daylight. One by one, they came up from the buried farm and stood about, hazarding guesses as to the whereabouts of other farms across the frozen water, searching in vain for the darkness of a wall or the plait of smoke from a roof. Some of the men set off on skis and rough snowshoes, returning an hour or two later with burning faces to tell of drifts twenty feet deep, of huts vanished without trace, of lost streams, of waterfalls muffled and frozen into fantastic structures of ice . . .

At Hvannabrekka, it was no better. The blizzard had blown straight up the valley with such force that by the end of the storm the snow was up to the little window in the loft. Pétur and Gunnlaug had abandoned the cold, empty house and moved in with the others in the farm, where the byre was situated directly below the room in which the people slept and the animals' warmth did much for the people huddled together above.

During the earlier part of the winter, Pétur had been away for much of the time and so had not had an opportunity of approaching Jón about Sunnefa and Jens Wium. But now, thrown together with him by the storm, Pétur saw his chance. As if by accident, he found himself and Jón sharing one of the big fixed beds. On the first night, he said nothing. But the following night, an hour or more after they had all gone to bed, while the wind tore and buffeted against the house, he sensed that the boy was still awake and turned towards him.

★   ★   ★

Just the other day, when I was copying out Hans's quarterly accounts, I caught myself thinking how extraordinary it is, the effect that a woman can have on a man – and I mean a man of intelligence, a man who's got the education and perspicacity to see how things are and who knows what he really wants in the long run. I mean, just look at Hans – he's young, happily married, newly started in a good job; and a just, conscientious man too, a thorough Christian, in fact. And now look what's gone and happened to him this winter! He seems to have completely lost his head over this girl. Granted, she's a fine-looking girl – but what on earth can Hans want with her when he has a wife like Gudrún? And doesn't he realize that everyone's laughing at him over this? As for the girl, it's hard to say what she's up to – one moment you'd reckon she's just leading him on, the next day you'd think she almost hates him.

There was that occasion just after we'd all moved in together during the blizzard. There we were, packed into the kitchen for supper, when in comes Sunnefa and wants to get past Hans to her usual place on the bench. She might at least have let Hans try and get out of her way – but, no, she just pushed past him, pressing right up against him. And then Hans had to seize her to stop her falling over the bench. He looked really embarrassed. And as for Gudrún – you could see that she wasn't best pleased either.

The worst of this whole business with Sunnefa is that soon everyone's going to know about it. In fact, I happened to overhear one of the girls telling that fat fellow from Hvannabrekka, Gudjón, about it and you can be sure that he won't keep it to himself. But, as I say, there are other times when Sunnefa gives him such cold looks that the poor man scarcely knows where to put himself. The only hope is that the infatuation will pass. He wants to keep clear of her but just can't seem to help himself.

*   *   *

For three weeks the clear, freezing weather held the country fast. The supplies of dried dung, fish bones and turf that constituted the source of fuel had just begun to run low when, a week or so before the end of January, it suddenly became warmer and the arrival of dark, fat clouds gave hope of rain. But thirty-six hours later, after a tempestuous downpour, the clouds passed on and the frost returned. The result was that every small path or track that had been broken through the snow now turned into a treacherous chute of thick ice. Over the previous weeks, contact had been maintained between the farms by ski and, where the snow was packed frozen, by horse. But now skis were of little use and even the sturdy horses could no longer keep a steady footing. One or two of the more enterprising farmers fitted their beasts with frosted shoes and so got about but otherwise people simply gave up and simply waited for rain.

And so February arrived.

*   *   *

He's a rum one, that Pétur. You never can tell what's going on in that mind of his. To this day I don't really know whether he's one to watch out for or if he's as he says he is, a friend who'd like to see me out of my troubles. But after I took Gudjón down a peg or two by laying him out in front of the others, he wouldn't have much to do with me no more. So I've been on my own a bit these last few months. Anyway, when the sheriff here finds himself bedded up with me because of the storm and wants to start talking all private like, about how I was brought up and who my father was and whether I'd been happy as a youngster – why, it was more than I could do not to feel sort of friendly towards him. And yet . . . I don't know, you look at him and something inside you says, 'Watch it, lad! That one's not quite as straight as what he'd like to make out.' Now, I can't put my finger on anything particular – I've just got this feeling as he's up to some sort of mischief or other.

He starts talking about where I was born and I tells him that I'm

87

from a place called Geitavík – that's Geitavík in Borgarfjördur. And your father?, he asks. My father, sir, I never knew. You see, sir, he was a fisherman, Jón Hrafngrímsson he was, big and strong they used to say; but the month before I was born his boat got caught up in a squall off Glettinganes and went down in the roost there. So I never got to see him, sir. My mother, sir? Well, she was a good woman and my sister and me, we loved her, we did. What's that? No, sir, she's not alive no more . . . No, sir, she didn't die a natural death . . .

Now why should he want to go on about my poor mother like that, I wonder? She's been dead these seven or eight years now and, God knows, she never did nobody no harm. But there was certainly something he wanted to know – it wasn't just idle talk. Anyway, I finally got through to him that I didn't care to talk about it. So he let me be and soon enough he was off asleep. But I was left there in the dark with the snowstorm tearing around the house, I was left there thinking about my mother. You see, one of the reasons I didn't fancy talking about her to the sheriff is that I don't quite know how she died.

The thing is, I was only a lad of eight winters when she went. That day, Sunnefa and me were over at the next farm playing with the farmer's two boys when all of a sudden everyone comes running and starts being really nice to us like it were our birthday or something. They wouldn't tell me nothing at first. But I found out from Sunnefa that mother had been taken sick and that we couldn't go home just yet because she was too poorly to see us. We got given a piece of dried fish and butter, which we both reckoned not too bad if mother was just laid up in bed for a bit; but then word came that we were to hurry back home. They put us up on the horses' necks and rode us over at a fearful pace. But when we got there, I knew from the look on their faces that we might just as well not have hurried so. I remember us being taken in to see her when they'd laid her out. But I'd heard someone say something about the place we always used to call 'the old house' so I slipped out to see if this would give me the answer to everything I didn't understand. 'The old house' was the original farm building that stood on the other side of a little grassy hill. When I got there, I went in but, in my hurry, I slipped and fell flat on my back. There I was, sitting in a pool of something wet and at the same time aware of a strange smell that I didn't recognize. I went across to the window to see what it was that was on my hands and all over my legs. It was blood. I just stood there and screamed, again and again, somehow thinking that I'd been the cause of my mother's death. I think I was still screaming when they came and dragged me out . . .

Well, to be truthful, I can't say I remember too much of the next few days. Sunnefa told me later how I'd gone sort of dumb like, so they'd just put me to bed and let me sleep. Anyway, by the time I was myself again, my mother had been buried and everything cleared up – and in a way it all seemed so long ago that it was almost as if I'd dreamed it. For a long time after that, we hardly mentioned her at all: I think we just wanted to forget.

And as I lay there, letting these thoughts take me along with them, I started off thinking of Sunnefa again. Apart from the sheriff's breathing next to me, I felt quite alone in the storm. And I knew as how Sunnefa would be feeling that way too, over in the other sheriff's place at Hjardarhlíd. It was as if all the other people just didn't count no more. And I began to think of how there was only six months before the ride to Thingvellir and how I could get to see her before then. And then I thought of as how it couldn't be more than a couple of hours' walk between her and me. When would this bloody snow go? When would I get a chance of seeing her again? How could we manage it? But then a voice in my ear was saying, 'Hey now, Jón! You'll need to stop that mashing and turning if either of us is to get a night's sleep.'

*   *   *

It was the end of March before the snows really began to recede. At last, the rains came and, day after day, their ranks passed across the valleys and hills, gradually eating away at the vast quantities of snow and ice that had built up in the first three months of the year.

By now, Jón could think of little but his need to see Sunnefa again. The way down the valley was open and it was often in that direction that he gazed – though he knew that it would be pointless to try and get to see her at Hjardarhlíd. He thought of going to Pétur and asking for his help, for the sheriff and he had had several more conversations since that night during the blizzard. But how could he ask him when Pétur's duty would oblige him to refuse? He thought of Gudjón, who often went over to Hjardarhlíd. But Gudjón was no friend of his and Jón saw little safety in entrusting him with a message. He would have to find some other way . . .

*   *   *

April 3rd 1741

No luck with S and JW yet. But I've got J where I want him. The young goat will run when I tell him. But must settle G first.

*   *   *

Jón had just finished clearing out the byre when Pétur called him over. Wiping his hands on his breeches, Jón walked through the mud to the main building.

'Come and give me a hand fixing the pen.'

'Well, sir, I'll need to get the smoke-house roof done first. I was told as I had to have that done by noon.'

'Leave the roof. I'll explain to them about that.'

They rode away from the farm and down the valley towards the pen that stood under the hill. Jón handled his horse well. Pétur watched him and saw too how his face set as he stared towards the Lagarfljót.

'I had some news from Hjardarhlíd the other day,' said Pétur casually.

Jón looked around at him. He knew nothing of deceit.

'How is she?'

'She's well, Jón. She's very well . . . But there seems to have been some trouble between her and Sheriff Wium.'

'How do you mean, sir?' he asked sharply.

'Well,' said Pétur with a little laugh, 'he seems to have taken a fancy to her.'

'Why, the bloody bastard, I'll . . .'

'Yes,' said Pétur, seizing the opportunity and speaking in a low, urgent voice as he rode up alongside the boy. 'Yes, it seems as if he can't take his eyes off her – and perhaps his hands too, for all I know. You can imagine what it was like when they were all crushed together night and day in the farm . . .'

Jón threw him off and spurred his horse down the track. It was several minutes before Pétur caught him up.

'Jón!' he shouted. 'Jón! Wait a moment!'

90

'I'll beat his brains out, I will!'

'Jón, wait! I've got a better idea,' shouted Pétur.

The boy slowed his horse and the two of them stopped and sat there panting for a moment before Pétur spoke.

'Look, you'll do yourself no good, rushing over to Hjardarhlíd like that . . . No, listen – firstly, why don't you speak to Sunnefa and find out if it's true?'

'And how the hell do I get to see her there?' Jón asked angrily.

'Now just listen to me. Do you know where Axlir is?'

'Axlir? Well, I've heard it spoken of. Isn't it up that way somewhere?' he asked, pointing back to the hills beyond Hvannabrekka.

'Yes, that's right. Now the normal way of getting there is by crossing the river down at the ford and then going all the way back up the other side. But there's another way. Look,' he said, taking the boy by the arm and turning him round till he faced back up the valley. 'You see the ridge up there on the right? Well, at the southern end there's a gap, a small pass, through which you can take a horse. Now when you get through the pass, you go straight on over the top till you come down to the river which runs through a gorge there. Well, between the head of the gorge and the first waterfall above it, there's a sort of bridge. It's only a rough thing made out of rope and a few boards – so you'd have to leave your horse there. But once you're over, you just go a bit west of north and after about a mile you come to Axlir. Do you follow me?'

'But what's all that got to do with me and Sunnefa?'

'Well,' replied the sheriff, looking him straight in the face, 'there's an old bothy at Axlir. Just up on the slope above the big marshes. Nobody ever goes there except during the autumn sheep-gathering. You could be on your own up there.'

'But how would I let her know?' asked the boy.

'Well, I might be able to get a message to her for you,' said the other man slyly.

'When?'

'Now wait a minute. There's something you've got to do in return. Ask Sunnefa about this business with Sheriff Wium. Ask her why she hated his father so much,' he added.

'What's that got to do with it?' said Jón.

'Look, if I'm to get you off at Thingvellir, you've got to help me by getting me this information. Right?'

91

'Right,' said Jón sullenly, not understanding what possible con-
nection there could be between the two things.

'And there's one other thing, Jón,' said Pétur darkly, dropping
his voice. 'I think your sister may be in some danger from Sheriff
Wium. So give her that knife of yours and tell her always to keep it
on her. And that if he ever tries anything with her, that she's to use
it. Promise me that.'

'I will sir,' said Jón, with a grin. 'I will that.'

The sheriff smiled.

Later that same day, Jón, walking out of the byre in a hurry, came
upon Pétur and Gudjón talking together. When they saw him, they
fell silent. Pétur smiled but Gudjón looked at the ground as the boy
went past.

★   ★   ★

Axlir was the name given to the rounded hill that rose from the edge
of the upland marshes, though it referred as much to the bothy
which stood under the hill. Built into the hillside, this was a rough
construction, with walls of turf and stone, and a driftwood frame-
work carrying the turf roof. Over each of the two doors was a small
window. This bothy was on the westernmost limits of the land
farmed by the people in that part of the country. For beyond it,
westwards, were the great inland wilderness of the Ódádahraun and
the ice masses of Vatnajökull, which together stretched a hundred
miles and more. It had that feeling of extreme remoteness, of being
on the very edge of the world, which brought to the men who visited
it a strange sensation of peace and awe.

It was one of those days of soft light and small breezes which come
at the end of winter, marking the point when the year's tides briefly
hang still before the surge of spring. The midday sun lay thinly
masked by flitches of high cloud. A skitter of wind moved piecemeal
from pool to pool among the marshes. Far off, a fox padded along
the back of a low ridge, seen only by a pure white gyrfalcon that
sprinted and jinked and then was gone as it swung round the edge
of the hills.

In the bothy, the boy and the girl lay together on the mound of
hay. The place was a warren of darkness and shadows, impaled by
two rods of gleaming weakness from the high windows. Only vague
shapes could be seen – the line of a rafter, the bulk of a wooden

stall, a coil of rope – but this was how they liked it to be for here they could hide from their separation and their misery. Here, in the cover of this false night and lulled by the sounds of the wind and the snipe and the first of the summer whimbrels, Jón and Sunnefa were briefly close to happiness.

'Hey, Jón!' she said quietly.

'Sunnefa!'

The wind rose from the marshes and ruffled the mane of the horse that stood tethered to a post by the bothy. And then the sun, too, broke free and, moving out from behind the clouds, shone down through the wind over the high wetlands.

It was mid-afternoon when he finally put her on her horse for the journey back to Hjardarhlíd. He stood by her side and took her hand.

'Now you'll get back all right, won't you?'

She smiled and nodded.

'You're sure as nobody knew you came up this way?'

She smiled and shook her head.

'And you won't forget what I said? You've got the knife?'

She smiled and nodded.

'Well then,' he said, looking down, 'till noon on Saturday.'

'Till noon on Saturday, Jón,' she said and rode off.

He watched her till she was out of sight and then, closing the bothy door, set out for Hvannabrekka.

*　　*　　*

April 8th 1741

So that was it! At last I know! And J tells me that her hatred for JW makes her feel the same way about HW as well. The poor fool tells me everything now as he needs my help in getting back up to Axlir. Ah, father! If you were only here! The sweetness of justice! But I must keep calm. G is my man. Lord be with me!

*　　*　　*

Lord help me! I fear I've no strength left. I make my wife miserable and my sister ashamed and now my mother has started on at me. 'Hans,' she says, 'you must take a grip on yourself. Think of others a bit more.' God Almighty! She asked me first if I were feeling all

93

right – she clearly thought I was sickening. And when I said I was healthy enough, she surmised that it was just some sort of moodiness. O God that it were! But how am I going to fight this longing I have for the girl? I swear that I shan't harm her. I swear it; yet at the same time don't know how I dare to do so . . . That Jóhann has started coming here again. God damn it!

★　★　★

There was a man called Eiríkur Gudmundsson who farmed at Höskuldsstadasel up at the other end of the Lagarfljót. As well as farming, he was spoken of as a first-class blacksmith. He was still in his youth and was broadly built though on the short side.

Eiríkur had been visiting Hjardarhlíd since the summer and it was widely said that he was interested in Gudný. On the Thursday morning of that week in April, he set out from home and rode along the bank of the Lagarfljót. When he came to Tó, he was invited in by Jóhann who suggested that they ride over to Hjardarhlíd together, when they had had something to drink. Eiríkur accepted this gladly.

★　★　★

'Excuse me, sir, but could I have a word with you?'

'What's that?' said Hans, taken by surprise and looking down at the fat man.

'Well, perhaps you don't know me, sir, but I'm Gudjón – from Hvannabrekka.'

'Yes, yes, I know you. You come over to see one of the girls here, don't you?'

'That's right,' the man replied.

'Well, what can I do for you?' said Hans, trying not to look impatient.

'Well, you see, it's like this, sir. I don't want to be thought a busybody or anything like that but I don't like seeing things being done that oughtn't to be done if we're to keep this country a good place to live in . . . if you follow me . . . Now I'd much rather it wasn't me that had to tell you because if anybody were to find out . . .'

'What are you trying to say?' interrupted the sheriff.

The man looked at him quickly out of the corner of his eye.

'Well, sir, it's just that that girl and her brother are meeting, sir. I thought you'd want to know, sir,' he added hurriedly.

'Sunnefa?'

'Yes, sir.'

'But how do you know, man?'

'Please, sir – not so loud.'

'How do you know?' repeated Hans in an urgent whisper.

'I just do,' he answered sullenly.

'Where?'

'Up at Axlir.'

Hans nodded slowly.

'They'll be going there on Saturday next. An hour before noon or a bit earlier.'

'Are you quite sure about this?'

'Oh yes, sir.'

They stood together in silence. Hans was lost in thought. The man looked nervously about.

'Well, I'll be on my way then, sir. I just thought I'd let you know.'

Hans nodded absent-mindedly as the fat man walked away.

*   *   *

Eiríkur and Jóhann rode up to Hjardarhlíd in the early afternoon. Both of them were in good spirits. Eiríkur asked Jóhann if he would be riding back that night.

'No, I'm planning to ride over to Brú in the morning.'

'It'll be pretty wet up in the marshes.'

'I'd rather risk a soaking than go all the way round by Jökuldalur,' said Jóhann cavalierly.

'Well, you'll need to mind how you go, all the same,' replied Eiríkur.

Jóhann went off to find Sunnefa; and Eiríkur, having talked for a while with Gudný and Gudrún, asked if Hans were busy. At this, Gudný looked away into the fire but Gudrún told him to go through and see Hans, who was in the study.

Eiríkur met Einar in the passageway.

'I'm just going in to see Hans,' said Eiríkur.

'Ah . . .' said Einar hesitantly.

'He's not busy, is he?'

95

'No . . . But you'd be best leaving it to another day unless it's important.'

'It is important,' answered Eiríkur, suddenly feeling irritated, and pushed his way past the secretary.

He walked through and banged on the study door.

'Who's that?' said a thick voice from inside.

'It's me – Eiríkur.'

'Oh . . . Come in then . . .'

When Eiríkur went in, he saw immediately that Hans had been drinking. Not by any bottles or flasks but from that slight slowness in his eyes, that dulled edge to his speaking as if his lips were frozen. Eiríkur's first instinct was to forget the whole purpose of his visit. But urged on by the thought of Gudný and also by a certain degree of plain obstinacy in his character, Eiríkur came quickly to the point.

'Hans, I've come to ask for Gudný in marriage. She knows my feelings for her and I'm hoping she'll not refuse me.'

Eiríkur, who was a good ten years older than the sheriff, had not particularly relished the idea of asking the younger man for what he thought could easily have been settled between Gudný and himself; but he knew the girl's regard for her brother and so had made himself go about it in the traditional manner. He imagined that Hans would be flattered by this gesture and would quickly turn the decision over to his sister.

But Hans sat there without saying a word, turning the silver ring round on his finger.

'Well?' said Eiríkur finally. 'Haven't you anything to say?'

'Look, Eiríkur, not now. Couldn't we talk about this some other time?'

But Eiríkur, until then unaware of how much he resented his position in this conversation, took this casual dismissal badly.

'And what's wrong with now?' he said indignantly. 'It's not that complicated a question, you know. You've only got to say "yes" or "no".'

'Eiríkur! Come on, don't pick a fight with me. I'll let you know one way or another in a day or two when I've had time to think things over.'

But by now Eiríkur was feeling angry and thoroughly obstinate.

'No – I'm not moving from here till I get an answer.'

'God Almighty! Can't you leave me be?' shouted Hans.

'When I've got my answer, certainly,' replied Eiríkur coolly.

Hans brought his hand down sharply on the desk and stood up.

'Right then – my answer is "no".'

'Why?'

'Because I say so.'

Eiríkur walked out, slamming the door behind him. He went straight out of the house, got on his horse and rode off home.

When Gudný came to see Hans a few minutes later, the first thing he said was:

'Is Jóhann Thorvardsson here?'

'Yes,' said Gudný, 'and he's staying the night. He's got to ride over to Brú in the morning . . . Hans,' she went on, hardly noticing her brother's distant look, 'what did Eiríkur want?'

'What? Oh, just some business or other . . .'

'He came to ask for me, didn't he?'

'Yes,' answered her brother, looking up at her sullenly.

'And you refused him?'

'Yes.'

'What reason did you give him?'

'I didn't. You didn't want him, did you?'

The girl paused; then shook her head.

But Hans was not to be so easily forgiven. All evening, both Gudrún and his mother took him to task over what he had done, saying that Eiríkur was a good man, that Gudný would certainly have grown to like him. Eventually, Hans took refuge from them in his study, where he once more began to drink.

The next day came with wind and low cloud, with bursts of drizzle that raked the river valley. But by the middle of the morning, the clouds began to clear and from time to time a watery sun broke through.

Without telling anybody where he was going, Hans fetched his horse and rode off. Half an hour later, in spite of warnings from the older folk who said that the marshes were a bad place to be caught in mist or cloud, Jóhann set off for Brú, which lay some forty miles away to the north-west. As he pointed out, the short cut he was taking involved only a stretch of five miles or so over the marshes and the route was well marked by cairns. He laughed at their needless worrying and rode off.

Hans came back not long after, saying that he had been up to

Hvannabrekka to see Pétur about the coming district assembly. But he was still in a sullen mood and soon went off to his study.

It was just past noon that the sky once more clouded over and it began to rain. But, unlike the early morning weather, the dense cloud now settled firmly on the hills and the drizzle continued unbroken for the rest of the afternoon. The hours passed dismally, with Hans and his family quiet and cheerless in the aftermath of the previous evening's quarrel.

But at about five o'clock, just as the light was beginning to thicken and everyone was preparing for the evening, the handful of people in the kitchen looked up as the sound of horses was heard outside. The door opened and one of the local farmers appeared, asking for Jóhann Thorvardsson.

'Oh, I'm afraid you've missed him,' they told him. 'He was away north earlier today.'

'Well, that's strange,' said the man. 'I've got his horse outside.'

'How do you mean? He was on his own horse this morning. The one with the fancy saddle.'

'That's just it. It was by the saddle that I knew whose horse it was,' said the farmer. 'I was coming back down Nordurdalur about an hour ago when all of a sudden the horse appears out of the mist. As far as I could tell, it was coming south – down off the marshes.'

'Oh God!' said one of the old women, 'something's gone and happened to him. We warned him, didn't we? He just wouldn't listen.'

It was agreed that there was no point in setting out to look for him until the morning but that a party would leave as soon as it was light. The farmer said that on his way home he would pass the news on to the other farms: they would need as many as possible if they were to stand a chance of finding Jóhann.

During the night, the winds and rain died away; and at dawn, the sky was clear. At sunrise, however, when the men gathered outside the farm, patches of dense mist could be seen lying over the wet ground of the marshes up on the heights above Nordurdalur. But, thinking of Jóhann and the night he must have spent, they knew that they could not afford to wait for the mist to disperse. Each man had his provisions, his flask of sour whey and water, his stick and his rolled blanket; and some of them carried rams' horns, to blow as a guide in the mist. Reaching the ford, they met other men from the far side of the water; so that by the time they came to the narrow mouth of Nordurdalur, the search party consisted of some fifteen riders.

★   ★   ★

'Jó—hann! Hey, Jó—hann!'

The long call floated through the thickets of mist that lay motionlessly on the marshes, floated through the morning stillness to where Sunnefa stood, wide-eyed and breathless, by the bothy door. Almost immediately, from another quarter of the mist, there rose the mournful belling of a shepherd's horn. The flat sound was drawn out but, before it had fully died away, other horns flared in answer and wove a mesh of dissonance over the hidden land.

Sunnefa had waited for an hour or so after the men had left and then, telling one of the old women – who were supposed to keep an eye on her – that she was going for a ride up the Lagarfljót, she had taken a horse and set out along the edge of the water. Once out of sight of the farm, however, she had turned up the course of a mountain stream and, a thousand feet higher, had come out on the rim of the marshes, where she doubled back above Hjardarhlíd and made for Axlir.

She had moved on cautiously, aware that at any moment she might meet up with the search party. And indeed, she soon caught sight of them, though only briefly, there and then gone again in the mist. Once she had passed where the track for Brú cut out into the marsh, she felt herself free and able to press on quickly for the bothy. At one moment, however, as she passed across the top of a gully, she was startled by a movement on the hillside below her. She was sure of it; but though she reined in her horse and sat peering down into the valley, she saw nothing more.

At Axlir, the bothy stood just clear of the mist, which lay lapping like some vast, unworldly sea against the foot of the slope. The sunlight, though still wintry and weak, filled the mist with a pearled glow; elsewhere, it caught at pools and put brightness in the dewy grass. Overhead, there was nothing but the breadth of blue.

Standing there, hearing the voices and horns drifting away in the mist, Sunnefa felt her calm return. She wondered again why Jón had needed to change the time, especially when it had meant entrusting a message to that unlikeable man, Gudjón. Then, scanning the hills for any sign of Jón, she fetched water and went into the bothy to wash.

99

Afterwards, she lay back in the hay and closed her eyes. She smiled to feel the broad beam of sunlight from the window falling across her bare body. All of a sudden the sound of the men out on the marshes had vanished; now she felt only the sense of freedom and peace, and a joy in her nakedness, the coming of spring after the long months of winter . . .

A bump sounded on the roof above her. For a moment she thought she had imagined it and so went on lying there, though now alert. But when she opened her eyes, she gave a small cry and reached quickly for her clothes: a man's face, upside down and against the sun, had been at the window above the door.

'Jón?' she called. 'Is that you, Jón?'

The door slowly opened. Sunnefa stood rooted, clutching her dress.

'Sunnefa? What are you doing up here?' said Hans, ducking in through the small doorway.

Sunnefa fumbled in her clothes for the knife. Hans was standing there quite still, staring at her.

'Don't come any nearer, Sheriff Wium. I warn you!'

Neither of them moved.

'Get your clothes on, child,' he said eventually in a quiet voice. 'I'll wait for you outside. You're coming back home with me.'

He walked out, closing the door behind him. Sunnefa began to dress; but before she had finished, the door opened again.

'I'm almost ready,' she said sulkily.

But a movement behind her made her turn. All she saw was the large figure coming at her and then she was being borne down into the shadows of the stall. Winded, she gasped out under the weight of him; and fought desperately as her skirt was pulled roughly up over her arms and face. Pinned in the darkness, with an arm heavily across her throat, she could only twist and turn. But already a knee was between her legs and the strength of him was too much. She cried out once, in rage, but he forced her head further back, into silence, and took her.

Later, he grunted and got up. When Sunnefa slowly pulled down her skirt from her face, he was standing there with his back to her, his head on his chest, his hands gripping the wooden stall. She looked blankly at him, saw his hands, his broad back and the way the sunlight shone on the shoulder of the heavy green coat that Gudrún had made for him in the autumn . . .

'Sheriff Wium!' she said hoarsely.

The man pushed himself away from the stall and walked out. She heard horses moving off and then once again the bothy was filled with the soft, impenetrable silence. She lay there with her eyes dull and still, waiting for tears to come.

For half an hour and more she lay there, with the strake of sunlight moving slowly up across her and the occasional cry from one of the men out on the marshes sounding in the distance. From time to time the whistle of a redshank was heard – but otherwise the sunny, upland silence was complete. She knew that she ought to move, to do something; but there seemed to be no strength left in either her will or her body.

But at last, as she lay still tearless and numb, staring up into the roof, she heard Jón arrive.

'Sunnefa! What is it? What's happened?' he said on seeing her.

She looked up vacantly at him as he crouched beside her; then reached up and brushed the hair from across his face.

'For God's sake, Sunnefa, tell me! What is it?'

But she would only look away and shake her head.

It was after they had been sitting there for some time that she finally spoke.

'Sheriff Wium,' she said under her breath.

'What about him?'

'Why were you so late, Jón? Why didn't you come before?' And then it came, the release of tears, overtaking her so violently that she almost seemed to be butting at the boy's chest as he held her.

Much later, when it had all drained from her, she told him.

'He forced me, Jón. Sheriff Wium forced me.'

'He what?' shouted Jón, jumping back. 'He . . . he . . . I'll kill him, by Christ, I'll bloody kill him!'

'No, Jón, listen, please listen! Promise me this, give me your word that you'll not do anything silly! We're in enough trouble already – you wouldn't stand a chance. Look, it seems that this other sheriff, Pétur Thorsteinsson, is friendly towards you. Go back and tell him everything. They say he's got no love for Sheriff Wium. He'll know how to help us.'

They talked for a while of what Jón was to tell Pétur. Then Sunnefa frowned.

'But, Jón, why were you so late?'

'Late? I wasn't late – it was near enough on noon when I got here. Just as we'd agreed.'

101

'Noon? But we were to meet an hour before that. You sent that message.'

'I sent no message.'

'I don't understand . . .'

When they came out of the bothy, the sun had cleared much of the mist. About a mile away to the east, a group of horsemen could be seen.

'What are they up to, I wonder?' said Jón.

'Oh, they're out looking for Jóhann. They think he may've got lost on his way over to Brú yesterday.'

'Who's Jóhann?'

'Oh, just one of the farmers. I never had much time for him,' replied Sunnefa.

*   *   *

Pétur wiped some of the mud from his boots and waited for his pulse to settle. Then he opened his journal and began to write. When he had finished and was waiting for the ink to dry, he went over and stood at the window.

He watched the boy bring his horse skilfully down from the ridge. The steep hillside was awash with bright sunlight and he could see every movement of horse and rider as they came plunging downwards. Pétur smiled and sat down again. He sniffed and looked at the open book in which he had just been writing.

April 13th 1741

This unexpected turn of events may well prove to be a better solution than I could have hoped for. I do not find it pleasant to consider what has had to be done in the interests of justice – but we are taught that the Lord works in strange ways.

He nodded in approval of what he had written and sighed. He got up and went back to the window. Jón was riding at full speed across the flat ground of the valley's head. Pétur watched him in satisfaction and then, as the boy drew near the house, he stepped back out of sight and, sitting down, began to read from the Bible.

But his eyes merely skimmed over the pages. He heard the horse pass, the boy cry out something as he dismounted and then the house door being roughly opened. A moment later Jón had burst into the room and was standing breathlessly before him.

'Here now, Jón, what's all the hurry? Can't you see I'm busy?' he said, holding up the Bible.

He looked down again to the book as if expecting the boy to retire.

'Look, sir, the Bible's the Bible and I don't expect that it'll change much one way or another in the next few minutes, will it? Couldn't it wait, sir? Sir, I've got to speak to you.'

Pétur put the book down with a look of benevolent indulgence. For all that he was a large, brutish sort of man in appearance, he knew how to give the impression of kindness.

'Well then, boy, you'd best close the door and then say what you've got to say.'

Jón's childish impetuosity had now gone. When he had shut the door and come back to stand in front of the sheriff's desk, his face had such a cold intensity to it that the glimmer of amusement which had appeared on Pétur's face faded away.

'Sir, you've got to help me.' This was said as a simple statement.

Pétur nodded slowly.

'I'm sure I'll do what I can.'

'Well, sir, it's like this . . . My sister went up to Axlir this morning like we'd planned. Only she got there a good while before me because of a message that some fool had gone and given her. For the life of me I can't think who can have done it. But that's not the point . . . though in some ways it is, like, for none of this would've gone and happened if she hadn't been early. The point is that that black-hearted bastard, that Sheriff Wium, followed her up there and . . . and . . .'

'And what, Jón?' asked Pétur calmly. 'And what, Jón?'

'And . . . well, sir . . . he ravished her.' The boy's voice had fallen low.

'Are you sure, boy?' asked Pétur fiercely. 'Do you know what you're saying? It's a very serious charge to make against a county sheriff.'

'I know what I'm saying, sir. Oh, he did it all right, the bastard,' he said with feeling.

Pétur was staring down at the desk, distant in thought.

'Are you going to help, sir?' asked the boy when the sheriff showed no sign of speaking. 'I told my sister as you were a friend.'

'Help you what?' he replied, looking up angrily. 'Help you try

103

and ruin the life of my colleague, a fine man at that, on the evidence of something that neither you nor I witnessed and which nobody can prove? And just to satisfy your lust for vengeance . . . No, I am not. I've been appointed a sheriff, not some kind of hired assassin. And my position as sheriff demands that I seek one thing only – justice. Justice for you, for Sheriff Wium and for everybody, including myself. No, for the moment I'm going to help you in something else – namely, to keep a tight control on yourself so that nobody knows anything about what's happened. Then, when I see fit, we'll find out where justice lies – and the necessary steps will be taken. And don't let me hear you referring to me as "a friend" again. I'm not your friend. I'm nobody's friend. I'm a sheriff and I stand alone.'

'But . . .'

'But nothing, boy!' shouted Pétur. 'If you want my help, you'll do as I say. Understand? I don't want you mentioning this to anybody. Now get back to your work and let me think. Go on! Off with you!'

'Yes, sir,' mumbled the boy dejectedly and went out.

When he had gone, Pétur stretched his arms lazily and sat back in his chair musing.

*   *   *

The old women stood at the door with hand-lamps while the men unsaddled their horses.

All day the party had ridden backwards and forwards over the marshes and had found absolutely nothing except a single, human ear. As this was discovered in a place where the ground was always a squall of mud, there was no way of knowing just what had happened. Two of the party were sent on to the farms on the other side of the marshes to see if Jóhann had ever got that far. Late in the afternoon, they came back, saying that nobody had seen him; but that they had found Skarphédinn Gudmundsson sitting drinking coffee with one of the farmers. Now Skarphédinn, a man from across the Lagarfljót, was known to have sworn that he would get even with Jóhann, who had tried to turn his wife's head. And Skarphédinn had come across the marshes the same day as Jóhann . . .

But, in any case, was it possible to identify a single ear? It was thought that Sunnefa might just recognize it: so that evening, one of the men casually placed it on the table in front of her.

'Do you happen to know whose that is?' he asked bluntly.

But Sunnefa just threw herself back from it and, running out of the room, would have nothing to do with it.

Was it Jóhann's ear? And if so, was he still alive, or buried somewhere in the marshes? Or maybe he'd never even gone that way after all . . .

★   ★   ★

It was the night of the new moon. Its delicate slice hung in a clear sky and cast the faintest of shadows round the buildings at Hvannabrekka. The two men spoke in whispers.

'Tell her to be there as usual, early afternoon, the day after tomorrow. Up behind the farm.'

'Right.'

'And, remember, you know nothing about all this for the moment. I'll tell you if and when I want the word sent round. Until then – nothing!'

'What's in all this for me?'

'Don't try that one again! You know as well as I do that if you so much as squeak about this, I'll have you before the court at the next assembly. You didn't think I'd forgotten, did you? But when this is all over, I might just give you something for your troubles.'

The look of irony on the face of the last speaker did not show in the shadows. The two men parted and went back to their beds.

★   ★   ★

As the winter fell behind and spring came slowly over the land, life at both Hvannabrekka and Hjardarhlíd went on at its normal, uneventful pace. For a while, Jón fretted about Sunnefa and thought much about vengeance; but became calmer when Pétur assured him that everything possible was being done to set things right. He asked Pétur if he could ride out to Axlir again, at which the sheriff threw up his hands at the boy's stupidity and explained once again that there must be absolutely no further contact between Sunnefa and him until the matter was settled.

At Hjardarhlíd, Hans was away for much of the time. If Sunnefa looked at him with hatred but never actually said anything, it was simply because she, like Jón, had put her trust in Pétur; and Pétur kept telling her, at their now regualr meetings, that an open confrontation with Sheriff Wium would do neither of them any good for the moment.

Spring passed and summer came. It was a day early in June, about a month before the opening of the Great Assembly, that Sunnefa met Pétur on the hill and told him the news which, for some time, he had been hoping to hear.

'Well,' she said with forced casualness. 'I'm pregnant.'

'You're sure?' he asked, looking hard at her.

She nodded and turned away, fearing that she was going to cry.

'Look, I'm sorry,' he said looking down at the ground. 'But try to think of it this way – now, at least, we've a better case. Are you prepared to name him and to say exactly what happened when the time comes?'

She nodded again.

'Please, can I see Jón now?' she said.

'No,' he answered with his thoughts elsewhere. 'Not yet.'

And then, almost overnight, every farm in the district was full of it. How Hans Wium, for all that he had shown himself to be a good sheriff, had gone and fathered a child on that Sunnefa. And as if it weren't enough that she was only seventeen and already under a sentence of death, she was actually in the sheriff's charge at the time. And then somebody else would put in that the girl, poor child, was not to blame – the brute of a man had raped her. What? Oh, but yes – didn't you know? Yes, he raped her up in the bothy at Axlir, the very day that the men were out looking for Jóhann from Tó. How do you mean, 'Can it be proved?'? Why, everybody knows that's what happened. Well, they'd heard it from – now, who had they heard it from?

But none of these details really mattered. The only thing of importance was that, by the end of June, the whole story had become accepted as fact among Hans's tenants. But as is often the case, Hans himself was the last person to hear about it. In the weeks since that fateful day when he had followed the girl to Axlir, Hans had done much thinking. Something very strange had happened to him up at the bothy. He told himself that he must have suffered some sort of black-out, for there was a part of that day of which he had no memory at all.

Then, one morning, Hans called Einar into his study.

'Einar, is everything organized for the ride west?'

106

'Yes indeed, Hans . . . But would you mind me suggesting something? Perhaps you shouldn't go to Thingvellir this year. Nor Sunnefa and her brother. I'm sure I can cope with the other cases on my own. As you know, they're only small matters.'

'Why on earth do you say that, Einar? I'd have to give Gudrún a very good reason for not going – I've promised her several things from Reykjavík,' said Hans laughingly, his green eyes narrowing. 'And why shouldn't Sunnefa and Jón go? It's imperative that we get their case cleared up. Einar, what on earth are you talking about?'

'Well, that's just it, Hans. I think that if you take them to Thingvellir, you'll not be doing their case any good. Nor your reputation, for that matter.'

'Einar, what are you trying to say?' asked Hans.

'Well . . . there's this stupid rumour going round at the moment . . .'

'Oh?' said Hans. 'And what's that then?'

Einar fiddled with the corner of the book he was holding.

'They're saying that the girl's carrying your child.'

'What?' exclaimed Hans.

'And that's not all, I'm afraid,' he went on. 'They're saying that you . . . you forced her, you assaulted her.'

'Sweet Jesu! And where's all this supposed to have taken place then?'

'I've heard them mention Axlir, Hans.'

The man buried his face in his hands.

'Hans – I don't believe a word of it. It can only be a story put about to harm you. But you must see that it'd be unwise to take the girl's case to the Assembly while this is in the air.'

Hans nodded slowly.

'Do the others know? My mother, my sister . . . and Gudrún?' he asked after a while.

'I couldn't say, Hans. I fear they must – there's been talk of little else for the past three weeks.'

'And why, in God's name, didn't somebody tell me?' burst out Hans.

'I'm sorry. I should have, I know. To tell the truth, I was just hoping the rumour would die out. The whole thing's a damned lie.'

'No, no, Einar, I'm not blaming you.'

Einar turned to leave.

'Oh . . . and Einar. We'll do as you said. I'll not be riding west.

Nor Sunnefa or the boy. You'll be able to handle the other matters, won't you?' said the sheriff wearily.

*   *   *

It was at the farm of Gaukshöfdi in February 1742 that Hans Wium was first officially faced with the accusation that he had raped Sunnefa Jónsdóttir and thereby fathered a child on her.

The previous summer, his sudden decision not to take the two accused to the Great Assembly had only served to strengthen the local belief in his guilt. Not long after Einar's conversation with Hans, the changing shape of Sunnefa's body had made it no longer possible for the people of Hjardarhlíd to pretend ignorance of what was being said. Gudrún turned on Hans, with anger and then cold silence, while Ingibjörg only mentioned the matter once, rebuking lightly, as if he had merely been a bit careless. After all the weeks of listening to the echoes of the rumour, neither of them really bothered to question the truth of it: it was only Gudný who asked him directly and with an open mind.

'It's not true, is it, Hans?' she asked one day during the hay-making.

'Of course not. But the way things are, I'd be hard put to find half a dozen men in the district who'd believe me. There's no point in denying it – I'm in a very uncomfortable situation.'

But there was little Hans could do. For he realized that if, at some later date, he was going to make a flat denial of any such charge, it would only be convincing if he had never shown any concern about the rumour. In any case, he asked himself, would Sunnefa actually try and name him as the child's father? Would she go so far as to accuse him of rape? The general opinion was that she would: but this opinion was held by people who already believed him to have committed the crime, while Hans himself knew the truth and knew that the girl must know it too. All he could do was wait . . .

In the circumstances, however, waiting did not prove quite so easy. He was now conscious that everybody was watching him; and, as the months went by, with the hay-making giving way to the autumn round-ups, and the days once more shortening, Hans began to feel the oppression of this isolation. Gone was the general ease of things, the feeling of sureness for the future; more and more he kept to himself, more and more did he struggle to maintain a public show of cheerfulness. And with the arrival of the winter darkness, he could no longer escape the sight of the girl, now large with child.

But one day in the middle of Advent, a month before Sunnefa's child was due, Hans sent Einar to fetch Sunnefa. He closed the door and told her to take a seat. She sat down, ill at ease, on the edge of the chair, with her hands in her lap and glowered at the sheriff. He stood looking at her for a moment and then, with a forced laugh, began to speak to her in an easy manner.

'Well, the child will be due soon enough now, won't it?'

She stared silently at him.

'Next month, isn't it?'

'You should know!' She thrust the words out through her teeth.

'Why do you say that?' he asked her, as he paced up and down.

'Sheriff Wium, you know just what I'm talking about! And if you don't, you will soon enough when the minister comes to see me next month for the church records.'

In spite of himself, Hans swung round and, walking smartly up to the girl, bent down to within a few inches of her face.

'Now look,' he said in a hushed but burning voice. 'I've heard the story that you've been putting about ever since last summer and I'm telling you here and now that if you persist with it, you'll end up in the Drowning Pool at Thingvellir. We both know that you were meeting your brother at Axlir. He's the father of the child – just as he was of the other. We both also know that I went to Axlir that day to bring you back and that . . .'

'Yes and what?' attacked Sunnefa. 'What happened then?'

'And that I never touched you!'

'Oh, I see! And would you mind telling me then who it was who came back into the bothy and raped me so that I find myself in the state I am now? Eh? Tell me that!'

'I don't know,' Hans replied, shaking with rage, 'but it was not me.'

'Well then, you must have a twin, Sheriff Wium,' she said ironically, 'whose wife also made him a nice winter coat out of green serge.'

There was a moment's silence while Hans struggled to let his anger settle. Then, going down on his haunches in front of the girl, he spoke to her in a gentler tone.

'Look, child – you and Jón stand under sentence of death. There is just a chance – a small chance – that the king in Denmark will see fit to have mercy on you, because of your ages. But if you insist on making this wicked accusation against me, you will certainly forfeit any hope of clemency.'

Sunnefa looked down and closed her eyes. But then she recalled Pétur's advice and, taking hold of herself, she looked up again at Hans.

'Sheriff Wium, on April 13th last, you assaulted me in the bothy at Axlir. The child I am carrying is yours.'

Hans stared at her sadly.

'Then, girl, you will end in the sack in the Drowning Pool. And your brother will lose his head under the axe,' he said coldly, standing up and walking away.

'No! Please! Don't let them do that!' she cried.

'Then tell only the truth!' he said, spinning round on his heels. 'Tell only the truth and I promise that I shall do everything in my power to save you.'

Hans saw himself neatly held. It was to be either Sunnefa and Jón, on a double charge of incest; or himself, on a charge of raping his ward. Was his belief in compassion to be knocked aside by his fundamental need to protect himself and his family? And, if it came to it, was he going to be able to take an oath on what had happened that day at Axlir?

But Hans was still pondering on all this when, in January, Sunnefa gave birth. When the child had been quickly passed to a wet-nurse, all eyes turned towards the track from Saudhagi, where Nikulás Hallgrímsson, the minister, lived. But it was to be almost a week before he came riding slowly down the way, stopping to talk and smiling amiably at everyone, as if unaware of the anticipation he was causing. He spent an hour or so at Hjardarhlíd and then rode home again, still smiling.

But for all his seeming equanimity, Nikulás Hallgrímsson knew that the church records must be kept complete if standards were to be maintained in the parish. So when Sunnefa, in spite of warnings and moral threats, had steadfastly refused to give him a name, he had gone straight to Hans and insisted that the matter go before a court of enquiry. By the end of that afternoon, there was not a farm in Fljótsdalur that did not know what had happened and that the girl was to appear at the court being held by Pétur Thorsteinsson a few weeks later.

And so it was that, early in February, on a wet, overcast day, the small court was held at Gaukshöfdi.

Sunnefa was clearly on edge. Her head was full of what Pétur had told her to do; and yet she was not able to forget her conversation with Hans. And, further down, beyond that, she was still oddly influenced by her first impression of the two men, that day many months ago on the banks of the Lagarfljót. For though Pétur now offered her advice and help, she was unable to escape the fact that the dark sheriff from Hvannbrekka inspired only feelings of fear and repulsion in her.

Pétur, by now quite confident that Hans's ruin was at hand, had told the district officer that he would be late and that the proceedings should therefore be started without him. He wanted it to be seen that no pressure had been put on the girl when she made her statement. In the event, this almost proved to be disastrous: for Sunnefa, in her confusion, had started by blurting out that Jón was the father. They asked her several times if she knew what she was saying and what the consequences of such a confession would be for her and her brother. She had just broken down and begged to be left in peace, when Pétur arrived. Sitting down, he looked at her fixedly and told her to calm herself. When there was complete silence in the room, he asked her who the father of her child was. There was nothing particularly threatening in his voice but his eyes never left hers.

'Sheriff Wium,' she said finally in a listless voice; and then added through the whispering of the court: 'He assaulted me on April 13th last in the bothy at Axlir. The child is his.'

After this had been accepted as her final statement, the court wanted to know only one other thing – why she had started by naming her brother. Pétur put this question to her.

'Well, you see, sir, I was frightened.'

'Of what?' asked Pétur with a kindness born of triumph.

'Of Sheriff Wium, sir. You see, sir, he told me that I'd be making a terrible mistake to accuse him of what he'd gone and done. He said all sorts of things to frighten me.'

'And inferred that since you'd already been found guilty of having a child by Jón, you might as well confess that this one was his too – as it would hardly make any difference . . .'

Sunnefa thought about this. She was not sure if this was true.

Hans had never actually said that. But perhaps he had been meaning that all along. Anyway, it was wiser to agree with Pétur.

'Yes, sir – that's right.'

By the time the court broke up, Hans Wium's reputation was ruined. To the charge of raping his ward was now added the shaming fact that, by threatening her, he had attempted to persuade the girl to perjure herself.

The case was deemed to be of such gravity that no district court could handle it. It was therefore decided that the matter, along with the earlier case of Sunnefa's first child, was to be put before the Great Assembly that summer.

*   *   *

'. . . and in the case of Arngrímur Magnússon of Sæhvammur in Bardarströnd, who has brought before this court an arraignment against Baldvin Halldórsson of Sandeyri in Patreksfjördur, that the aforesaid Baldvin did wilfully and maliciously cause the death of eight of the plaintiff's horses at the last autumn round-up at Vestur-botn in Patreksfjördur, it is deemed that the defendant is guilty and shall therefore pay the sum of three rix-dollars in compensation, which payment to be made before the first day of winter.'

As the magistrate's voice died away, discussion broke out among the throng of men. They were composed, in the main, of sheriffs and important farmers from all over the country; and they now stood packed into the court-house of the Great Assembly at Thingvellir. Many of them had travelled long distances to attend the Assembly, some because they had important lawsuits, and some simply because it befitted their status that they should be seen at the country's most important annual occasion. All the notable people had their own lodgings at Thingvellir, booths consisting of four walls of rock and turf, over which was drawn a simple covering of homespun cloth. Lesser folk, unless lucky enough to find shelter in somebody else's booth, had to set up their tents on the banks of the river. The court-house itself was merely a larger booth, with the walls support-ing a number of roof-poles for the thick covering, and each end of the building open to the drizzle and gusty wind that now blew.

The court clerk, seated at a small table, wiped his nose on the back of his hand and cursed as the rain once more splashed across the book in which he was writing. He thought bitterly of the answer

112

which the king's steward had given to their application for a proper court-house. He was very sorry, he had said, but there just wasn't enough money to cover the cost of the wooden building they were asking for – though he promised to see what he could do to have the existing one done up. Done up! thought the clerk. How could you do up a building which had large holes through which the weather came driving in, quite apart from a roof that leaked? It was all very well when the weather was fine, as it had been on the first two days of the Assembly; but when it turned wet, it was a miserable business sitting there hour after hour frozen and soaking . . . And as the page was sprayed yet again by the rain, he turned in exasperation to one of the magistrate's assistants and told him that unless he wanted a mere pudding of pulp and ink as a record of the court's dealings, he would have to get him some sort of shelter.

Over the noise of the general discussion, the hollow voice of the magistrate was heard again.

'For the third and final time, I call Hans Wium! Hans Wium, sheriff in Múlasýsla, please step forward!'

There was no sign of Hans. But a very small, lightly built man with pale skin and crimped, red hair limped forward. He was in his late forties and, although he only came up to the shoulders of most of the men around him, he gave off an air of complacency and self-assurance. His eyes were green and set close together. He leant on his stick and spoke lazily to the magistrate.

'I've been asked to speak for him.'

'Sigurdur Stefánsson, isn't it?' said the magistrate, looking down at the speaker without any great liking.

'Yes,' he drawled. 'That's right – sheriff in Austur-Skafta-fellssýsla. Sheriff Wium sent a message asking to be excused. He says that he's once again unable to attend, owing to the state of his county. They had famine and the smallpox earlier this year. He got the pox himself, apparently, but managed to pull through. How-ever,' he yawned, 'however, owing to the famine, poor Sheriff Wium couldn't get together enough horses to make the journey. No doubt he'll manage it next year.'

'A likely story!' said somebody acidly. 'It wasn't horses he couldn't get enough of – it was courage.'

All around, there was head-shaking and muttering at what was considered to be disgraceful behaviour from a sheriff. They certainly knew that Múlasýsla had had a famine and a bad outbreak of smallpox; but not one of them had any doubt that Hans Wium had once more failed to come to Thingvellir simply because public opinion was violently against him for what he had done to the girl Sunnefa.

The clerk, who was still waiting for his shelter to arrive, sneezed twice and, hawking loudly, began to add Hans Wium's name to the list of sheriffs not present at the 1742 Great Assembly.

*   *   *

God Almighty, if they'd only just leave me alone! But no – she and my mother are both on at me day and night, on and on, railing at me for not doing something to clear it all up. Somehow I forgive my mother: she's not been at all well since the last famine. But Gudrún, my dearest Gudrún, her constant anger with me brings me real grief. Clearly both of them are frightened that I won't be able to clear my name, that I'll be ruined, and them with me. But with Gudrún, there's something else as well – in spite of everything I've told her these past months, there's part of her that's still not convinced that I never touched the girl – and for that, she simply can't forgive me. At the same time, she knows, I think, that we can somehow get over this. The business of saving my reputation, on the other hand, she sees as something that can't wait another day.

First, she wants me to make a formal deposition that I was never at Axlir that day, that I was with her the whole time. And of course, I could do this easily enough. Just a quick lie before a court. What are a few words when they can restore happiness to a whole household?, she would say. But afterwards – how does one live with a lifetime's memory of perjury?

Then she wants me to get Eiríkur Gudmundsson to speak up for me. She says that as he's now a much-respected district officer, he could be of great help to us. I pointed out that he's not likely to feel particularly well-disposed towards me after the way I turned him down eighteen months ago. Just how was I supposed to win him round?

'Send Gudný to him,' she replied, without so much as a blink.

My own sister, as some sort of bribe! It's not that I ever really thought so badly of Eiríkur – but I simply refuse to start telling my sister whom she should marry, just so as to improve my chance of saving myself. No, if she ever went to him, it'd have to be of her own accord.

In all this, I've somehow got to keep before me that one's conscience is the only reliable yardstick of what is right. After all, which of us would care to have the world think him free, happy, maybe even admirable, when in fact he's rotten with shame?

I certainly shan't speak to Gudný about Eiríkur. Much as I love Gudrún and would like to see her happy, I can't surrender my beliefs just because of her. Isn't one a person first and a husband second?

*　　*　　*

Eiríkur stood stripped to the waist in the small smithy at Höskuldsstadasel and worked the horsehide bellows at the base of the fire. With the scarcity of good fuel, it needed a lot of experience and a certain knack to keep the fire at the right heat. He kept peering and stoking it, till the heart of the fire was ready; then, using the heavy tongs, he thrust the blade he was working into the glowing core. He watched the heat rise, step by step, into the metal; and as it touched the dull red of hardness, he drew it swiftly from the fire and quenched it in the bucket beside him. Steam clouded up, pluming around his head, transforming him into some mythological smith. It was at that moment, from out of his cloud, that he heard her speak.

'Hello, Eiríkur.'

He all but dropped the blade in his surprise.

'Gudný!' he exclaimed.

'Well, Eiríkur, I thought I'd come and pay you a visit – since you refuse to come and see me these days,' she added coquettishly.

'You know perfectly well why I haven't been to see you,' he said in a serious tone, walking her away from the furnace.

'You just caught Hans at a bad moment – that's all. And you never came back and asked me, did you?'

Eiríkur shook his head slowly and smiled. Then he turned and looked at her solemnly.

'So why now, Gudný? After all these months.'

For a moment, the girl dropped her eyes.

'It . . . it's been so long, Eiríkur. I wasn't sure how much longer I could go on waiting.'

She looked up and he was staring silently at her. She quickly put her hand on his arm and kissed him.

The day before the autumn round-ups began, Gudný and Eiríkur

115

were married at Höskuldsstadasel. At the wedding, Gudrún looked across the crowd of people and gave her sister-in-law a warm smile.

But for all this, the wedding did not go without mishap. Ingibjörg, who had been weak ever since the spring famine, had insisted on riding all the way from Hjardarhlíd without a rest and arrived looking exhausted. She joined in the festivities but later said that she would go and lie down for a while. Early that evening, when they went to fetch her, they found her lying dead in the bed.

The ride home after they had buried her was sad and silent. With her dead and Gudný gone, and with the case hanging over every thought of their future, there seemed little for Hans and Gudrún to say to each other. For by now they had reached a deadlock over the case, Hans still refusing Gudrún's demands that he should make a formal denial. They rode side by side along the Lagarfljót, each of them locked away in thought and unable to speak.

But Gudrún proved to be right about Eiríkur. He was a straightforward and dependable person, quite without the passions that may make for great men and usually ruin lesser ones. His general openness and his willingness to help had made him friends throughout the region: people, sensing that there was no duplicity or guile in him, tended to believe what he had to say. And once he was married, what he had to say regarding the sheriff's case soon began to follow his wife's adamant conviction of her brother's innocence – so that, over the weeks, local opinion on the matter first began to waver and then to turn away from the outright condemnation of the past months.

By the following spring, the feeling in Fljótsdalur, and indeed in that whole section of the county, was quite different. Travelling around in his work as district officer, Eiríkur had almost unwittingly achieved what Hans needed. The conviction with which he spoke about the matter had given many people not just a new opinion on it but more of a new belief. And as the news passed on its way among the farms, each re-telling of it gave it added certainty. So that by the time it had followed its full course and come back to Eiríkur, it had been strengthened by countless new details. Now the story was that the shameless girl had set out to blacken the sheriff's name, some saying to cover her own and her brother's guilt, others because the sheriff had rejected her advances.

When Hans rode out to his tenants and was greeted as in earlier days, with words of friendship and goodwill, he came home feeling sure that everything was now not lost. Gudrún smiled to herself to hear the news; and when next she went visiting at Höskuldsstadasel, she took with her an extravagance of presents. But they were not to be enough. For as soon as she arrived, she saw that not only had Gudný's lightness of spirit quite gone but that there was also a strong current of resentment in her behaviour towards Gudrún. The decision had been taken, those months before, in a surge of generous fervour; now, with the quiet passing of the days, the fervour had drained away – and Gudný remembered only from where the main persuasion had come. When the time came for Gudrún to leave Höskuldsstadasel, the farewell between the two of them was full of smiles and promises of future visits. But both knew that the fullness of friendship, which they had enjoyed before, was now dead.

* * *

Einar pulled the heavy, woollen blanket up round his shoulders and waited for sleep to come. He had been lying awake for several hours now, listening to the wind and the sound of a nearby stream. He thought to himself how glad he would be to get back to Hjardarhlíd the next day. He had had enough of this living rough that so many of the others seemed to enjoy. It was the best part of a month since they had left Fljótsdalur and the prospect of a proper bed and of days spent doing something other than riding made him glad that it was all nearly over.

The journey out had been bad enough, what with the endless rain and the girl in tears most of the time, but the return had been even worse. As soon as they left Thingvellir, back had come the gales and rain. And to cap it all, coming up over Vonarskard, they had been caught in a blizzard – yes, a blizzard, and only a month after midsummer! No, all this living in tents was not for him.

This final night out, however, they were in a little bothy, up in the hills to the west of Fljótsdalur. There were twelve of them dotted about in the hay-loft which filled one end of the building. Some of them were simply people from further east who had chosen to ride with the party from Fljótsdalur: but the two people in the bothy that night who interested Einar were Pétur Thorsteinsson and fat Gudjón from Hvannabrekka.

Deciding that he could no longer stand lying awake in the dark, Einar felt his way over to the ladder and climbed down from the

117

loft. Outside the bothy, the horses shuffled and snorted as he passed by in the warm half-light. He went up on to a hillock from where he could look out towards the bulk of the glacier, hazy pink in the vague, summer night. Sitting down and wrapping the blanket about him, he sat staring into the distance, half dozing, going back in his mind over the days at Thingvellir . . .

Yes, he thought, that was it – Pétur Thorsteinsson and fat Gudjón . . .

While Einar was not a suspicious man by nature, he was also not a fool. And in the week between the opening of the Assembly and the calling of Sunnefa's case, he found himself watching Pétur Thorsteinsson with the girl and her brother, and wondering at the sudden urgency in their conversations. For while Pétur had had the boy at Hvannabrekka all those months, Einar had always seen the case as belonging more, by inheritance, to Hans.

And through those long, warm days of waiting, a strange train of doubt mixed with suspicion had begun to evolve in Einar's mind. Stories he had heard of Pétur's father, of Pétur's cousin, lost just before their marriage, of Ingibjörg's hatred of the people at Hvannabrekka; and then Pétur himself, maybe not simply the dour, unsociable person that he seemed to be, maybe something more complicated, a little more involved . . . And Gudjón? What was the seeming collusion between him and Pétur? What indeed had brought him all the way to the Assembly? And what was the cause of that look of amused scorn, a real look of cruelty, on the fat man's face when he was talking to Jón . . . ? Where was the connecting line through all this?

Away to the north, the summer sun was beginning to rise into an open sky as the thoughts kept turning in Einar's mind.

*   *   *

After a delay of three years and eight months, the case of Sunnefa and Jón had finally been put before the court at the Great Assembly. Jens Wium's verdict given at Bessastadir in Fljótsdalur in February 1740 was upheld and the entry in the court records read as follows:

It is hereby deemed that Jón Jónsson and his sister Sunnefa Jónsdóttir, whose criminal association resulting in the birth of a child was brought to light in 1739, have, by this serious transgression

118

of the law, duly forfeited their lives, both of the aforementioned having freely admitted to their guilt, first before the district court and later before the court of the Great Assembly. The sentences are that the aforesaid Jón shall be beheaded while the girl Sunnefa is to be drowned. The sheriff for the central section of Múlasýsla is to be responsible for the carrying out of these sentences in accordance with the stipulations of the law. However, because of mitigating circumstances, namely their ignorance and the fact, established on November 22nd 1739 and confirmed by the church records at Desjamýri, that when this major crime was committed Sunnefa was no older than sixteen and her brother only fourteen, their case is first to be most respectfully referred to His Majesty's clemency. And while His Majesty's most gracious decision is awaited, the two condemned persons are to remain in the jurisdiction of the sheriff and not be handed over to the executioner.

July 17th Anno 1743

In the circumstances, it was considered unwise that the boy and the girl should be returned to Fljótsdalur and the court consequently decreed that while the king's decision was being awaited, they should both be put in the charge of other sheriffs – a good distance both from Fljótsdalur and from each other. Sunnefa was therefore handed over into the care of Sheriff Angantýr Atlason of Glúmsstadir in the district known as Land in Rangárvallasýsla; while Jón was assigned to the keeping of the man who had spoken for Hans Wium at the last meeting of the Assembly, Sheriff Sigurdur Stefánsson of Smyrlabjörg under Skálafellsjökull in the district known as Sudursveit in Austur-Skaftafellssýsla.

In the case of Sunnefa's second child, heard in the afternoon of the same day, she once again named Hans Wium as the father and continued to claim that he had assaulted her in the bothy at Axlir. However, numerous people from Múlasýsla who had come to the Great Assembly for the express purpose of seeing that Sheriff Wium was not wrongfully accused, spoke up on his behalf and repeatedly gave the court to believe that with his impeccable record and his fine, generous nature, it was most improbable, to say the least, that such a crime could have been committed by him. As the girl's record was far from perfect, any accusation made by her would need to be supported by strong evidence before it could be considered seriously. The court, clearly not sure that the matter was quite so simple, yet at the same time finding that there was insufficient evidence for a verdict, ruled that the case should be adjourned pending further investigations; but that Sheriff Wium should be fined ten rix-dollars for maladministration, for having failed to bring these two serious cases to the Great Assembly earlier.

The following day, July 18th, instructions came from the governor, Joakim Lafrentz, that Pétur Thorsteinsson was to oversee the investigations and that Sigurdur Stefánsson was to act as counsel for the prosecution. It was considered by all rather pointedly harsh of the governor that he should also instruct Sheriff Wium to pay the fine of ten rix-dollars to Sigurdur Stefánsson, to cover his costs in preparing the case for the prosecution.

On the morning of July 19th 1743, in bright sunshine and a high wind, Sunnefa and Jón said goodbye to each other. She was a month short of her twentieth birthday; he had passed his eighteenth only two days before. They would never see each other again.

The case surrounding the paternity of the second child had only just begun.

4

THE CASE OF SUNNEFA: 1743-58

West from the little village of Höfn, which stood perched on a spit of land in Hornafjördur, the flat land of the coast ran away south-westwards and became progressively narrower as it was squeezed between the Atlantic and the ice-fields of Vatnajökull. But even on this thin coastal belt, where rough hills of scree and shale and poor growth levelled out to the strip of grassland, once washed by the sea, men somehow managed to scrape a living. The farms, strung out in a line along the coast, lay tucked in beneath the slopes of the hills that climbed away in shattered ridges towards the snow above. Everywhere, the land was dominated by the glacier: snouts of deeply scored ice pressed stealthily down beside the farms before melting away in torrents that poured on towards the waiting sea.

On an afternoon in May 1748, nearly five years after the trial at the Great Assembly, a man was to be seen riding west through this narrow tract of land. He was tall and strongly built but his face was hidden for he had pulled a piece of cloth about his head in protection against the sandstorm that raged about him. He rode steadily but without hurrying, his back straight and his legs stretched forwards in the stirrups, giving him a look of unconcern as storming clouds of sand boiled over him and the spare horses. Between the squalls, the sand streamed hock-high across the flats so that rider and horses seemed to be passing through a vast ford of dust. There were no majestic views of the glacier that day, no wide panoramas of crested hills and ice. The sky was covered and every rock and hollow thundered with the wind. Three miles away, the long smudge of the sea was ragged with whiteness. Nobody rode out in weather like this unless their business was vital.

The man had left Höfn earlier in the day and, having passed by the farms of Mýrar, was now crossing the sands before entering the parish of Sudursveit. One of the first farms to be met on coming into Sudursveit from that direction was Smyrlabjörg, the home of Sigurdur Stefánsson, and by now the horseman was staring ahead and trying to penetrate the storm for a sight of the farm. He did not belong to this part of the country but knew it well enough to recognize that he was not far from the sheriff's house. A mile or so later, with the track now close up by the shore, he slowed his horses to a trot as Smyrlabjörg came into sight.

It was not, by any standards, a large farm. Just a row of four gable-topped fronts of wood, three with merely a door and a single window, and the fourth larger, with a door and three windows. A layer of turf ran up and down over the four ridge-poles to form one continuous roof. Unless one happened to know it was there, it was hard to discern from any distance – a mere serrated formation in the hillside, lacking even the paintwork of thermal mud which was used to brighten the buildings in other parts of the country.

When he arrived, there was no sign of life at the farm. Tethering his horses to a post, he knocked loudly at the door of the main building. Then, as there was no answer, he pushed open the door and went in, and found himself standing in the dim light of a corridor, with the storm's noise suddenly muffled and distant. Only now, seen against the perspective of the building's interior, did it become clear how large he was, for the proportions of his body had disguised his real size.

He drew the cloth from his head and, hearing a sound in a room close by, opened the door and walked in.

*   *   *

I suppose that it was only in the months following that meeting of the Great Assembly in '43, when I'd come back to Hjardarhlíd with the news of Hans's fine and the forthcoming investigation, that I first got to know Eiríkur Gudmundsson. His greatest asset, it always seemed to me, is that he's entirely genuine – and humble too. To talk to the man you'd have no idea of the standing he has in the area, for he seems quite ordinary and quiet, even a bit diffident. He sits there nodding and puffing at his pipe, interested in everything yet always making light of his own knowledge.

One day about nine months after the case had gone to the Assembly, I was sitting by the fire at Höskuldsstadasel on my way back from the fjords.

'If it weren't for the sheriff at Hvannabrekka,' said Eiríkur all of a sudden, 'I'd say the whole thing would die out within the year.'

'Why on earth do you say that?' said Gudný in that slightly testy voice she'd come to use with Eiríkur.

'Well, my dear, I suppose I remember better than you how things

122

were in your father's day. Pétur's father had no love whatsoever for Jens – and I don't think Pétur himself wants that forgotten. Whether it's all to do with the way his father died, as well as losing his cousin, I couldn't say.'

'But just the other day I was thinking how friendly Pétur had been to Hans and Gudrún this last month or so,' I said.

'Ah!' said Eiríkur, tapping out his pipe. 'I shouldn't be too convinced by that. I imagine that that's simply because he's sure that one way or another the case will still bring Hans down.'

'But how?' cried Gudný. 'How, when everybody knows he's innocent?'

'Of course everybody knows he's innocent. But there are other ways, you know. And Pétur's very full of hate. I don't think one should ever feel too sure about him.'

I rode back to Hjardarhlíd the next day wondering if Eiríkur was right about him. Certainly, he's considered a difficult man, fractious and moody, hard to please and slow to thank – but much of this is put down to shyness. There are also stories of him having a leaning towards religion, that he spends much of his time reading devout books – and, again, this seems to explain to people why he doesn't have any social life to speak of. That's just the way Pétur Thorsteinsson is, people say, and they find nothing queer in it. But the man's silence and his thin, cynical smile disconcert me, making me imagine things about him that I don't like . . . And since my talks with Eiríkur, there've come back to me the memories of that summer at the Great Assembly – memories that have now taken on a new and more sinister aspect. No – I'm convinced that Pétur's life is filled with something other than the shyness and holy books that people suppose. Eiríkur has suggested hatred. I'm not sure that I really believe this. But all one can do is to watch and wait.

In these four years and more since the investigation was officially started, almost nothing has happened. Hans is too fair a man to try and hinder a legal process, especially when it's against himself; but, since he's also not fool enough to help in his own prosecution, he's done his best not to know what's going on in the proceedings. During all this time, he's made no mention of the business; and, after the first month of shame over the Assembly's verdict, he's ridden out in the district and quite gone back to his old ways. The people like him. In spite of what some of them may have thought of him before the trial, they now sense that he can't be guilty. But these days

123

nobody talks about it much, though a satisfactory solution is clearly still needed.

It's not easy to guess what Pétur's been thinking all these years. To begin with, I imagined that the reason for the apparent inactivity of the prosecution was his unwillingness to be seen to be organizing what is basically an attack on a colleague. This fitted in well with the picture we all had of him as a shy man. But once I'd become suspicious, I began to keep my ears open and soon learnt that Pétur is far from timid about fulfilling his role as head of the investigation, that countless sealed letters have been carried south to Sigurdur Stefánsson and that replies have been few and far between. Of course, Pétur's hands are tied: he was appointed to oversee the investigation and no more. So all he can do is to put pressure on Sigurdur. Presumably, he would expect him to come east to Múla-sýsla – perhaps to Hvannabrekka itself – and to stay here until he had collected the necessary information. Until he can get the man to do that, he's got little hope of bringing Hans to trial.

At the beginning, it looked as if the case were going to be forced through quickly: the governor in those days, Joakim Lafrentz, showed himself very concerned about the matter. But, from early in 1744, Lafrentz's health took a turn for the worse. The consumption that'd been eating away at him for years suddenly got worse in the New Year. For another eleven months he managed to stagger on, drinking enormous quantities of red wine: but the life was out of him and he finally died the following Christmas.

From what we heard, one would've thought that his successor, Johan Pingel, had come to Iceland under protest. Even now, he seems to have little interest in our country. I suppose he just about fulfils all his duties – making a decision here, summonsing a man there – but he makes no attempt to be involved. By the time he arrived, Hans's case had lain dormant for a year and a half; and, though he must have known of its existence from Lafrentz's papers, he wasn't going to rake up something which might cause him extra trouble.

Hans's attitude towards Pingel is remarkable. He knows that if the governor cared to do so, he could easily insist on the case being brought to court. Yet, in spite of this, Hans is so conscientious in his duties as sheriff that when Pingel's idleness causes delays in the resolving of other matters, he fumes about the man's incompetence. Does some perverse part of him seek punishment?

Three years have now past since Pingel took over. There's every appearance of peace in Fljótsdalur these days. Hans and Gudrún seem to have got over their temporary difficulties. Hans works hard at his job. He rides out regularly with Pétur, who appears to have put aside any enmity he may have felt towards Hans in the past. Even the weather is good . . .

The last time I saw Eiríkur I passed the remark that his earlier prediction about Pétur had fortunately proved to be wrong. He looked at me through a cloud of pipe-smoke and said:

'I would never be happier to admit that I'd been wrong. But, Einar, what's four and a half years to a man in his early thirties? With a lifetime ahead of him and no other interests?'

He raised his eyebrows and pursed his lips round the pipe's stem in a look of enquiry.

'Don't you think you're exaggerating a bit, Eiríkur?'

'Perhaps, perhaps, my friend . . . But I can assure you that it'll be a long time before he gives up. But if you don't believe me, you ought to try listening to the talk in the farm at Hjardarhlíd.'

'Why's that?'

'Well,' he replied laughing, 'young Haraldur, one of the parish poor we took in here, is in some way related to that girl Sigrún at Hjardarhlíd.'

'So?' I said, still puzzled.

'Come now, Einar! Sigrún is a friend of Ragnhildur, the woman who's going with that man Gudjón from Hvannabrekka. Well, Haraldur tells me that from time to time Gudjón takes a bit too much to drink and says a few things to Ragnhildur . . .'

'. . . who tells Sigrún who tells Haraldur who tells you. Is that it?'

Eiríkur laughed again.

'Who tells you . . .'

I smiled.

'So what've you been hearing then?'

'That Pétur was in a foul mood last month. That he's just got back from Höfn and is now in much better spirits.'

'But what, in heaven's name, does that prove?'

'Prove? It proves absolutely nothing, Einar,' he said before dropping his voice to a more serious tone. 'But to me it suggests that at last Pétur has got something on the move with that fellow Sigurdur

Stefánsson. And Pétur's good spirits usually suggest bad news for Hans.'

★   ★   ★

Hans and Pétur were riding together to a session of the district court. Hans was cheerful and talkative; but Pétur, as was usual when he was with Hans, spoke little.

'Not bad weather we've been having,' said Hans lightly.

'No, not bad, I suppose.'

'Were you away last week?'

'Yes – for a few days.'

They rode on in silence.

'It'll have been windy in Höfn, I should imagine.'

Pétur hesitated for a moment.

'Yes, it was. But I was only there for a day.'

'Ah! Did you go on west then?' said Hans casually.

'What, you mean to Smyrlabjörg?' replied Pétur quickly, with a fine bite of malice in his voice.

'Well, no . . . I meant, did you . . . ?'

'No, I didn't,' interrupted Pétur. 'Why, was there a message or something you wanted taken that way?'

'No,' replied Hans sullenly. 'No, to tell the truth I was just wanting to know how young Jón was getting on. I must say, you'd have thought they'd have come to a decision about the pardon by now, wouldn't you?'

'Didn't I tell you? The pardon came through some time back.'

Hans reined in his horse and turned on Pétur.

'What? Why, in heaven's name, wasn't I told?'

'Well, I suppose that in the circumstances it was thought more fitting to inform me.'

'I still think you should've told me. But I'm surprised I didn't pick it up in the district. Who did you tell?'

'Well, I thought it best not to say anything until the . . . that is, the second case is concluded.'

Hans turned away, his face set in anger.

'But Sunnefa and Jón were informed, I hope.'

'I really don't know. I should imagine so. No doubt Pingel will have written to Sigurdur and Angantýr.'

'So they've been held since then purely for what you call the "second case"?'

'Yes.'

After a moment's thought, Hans rode on. Pétur followed him.

'And this "second case" – when's it going to be presented at the Assembly?'

'Oh, soon I hope. You see, it doesn't entirely depend on me. If it did, it'd all be over and done with by now.'

'I'm sure it would,' said Hans. 'And I'm equally sure you know what the verdict would've been too.'

'Now, Hans, how could I possibly know that?'

'Well, I'm beginning to be able to guess what you'd like it to be,' he said aggressively.

'What do you mean by that?'

After four years of silence on the matter, Hans now found himself unable to halt the anger that was rising in him.

'I mean that you don't care a straw for the wretched Sunnefa or her brother. That you've only one thing in mind and that it doesn't worry you in the least how long they are kept under arrest.'

'What are you talking about?'

'You know exactly what I'm talking about, damn you, Pétur!'

The man looked away from Hans's burning face.

'You're talking nonsense, Hans. All I want to see is justice.'

'Justice!' sneered Hans. 'And what do you know of justice? You're as bad as your father. He talked about nothing but justice while all the time . . .'

'Hans, shut up!' said Pétur coldly. 'Let's leave my father out of this, shall we?'

'And how on earth can we leave him out of it when he's the reason for the whole way you behave towards me?'

'The way I behave towards you? And what way's that then?' asked Pétur mockingly.

'Oh, come on, don't try and play the innocent with me!' snapped Hans. 'You may fool some people with that pious stuff about justice but it doesn't work on me. It's quite obvious you can hardly wait to see me brought down.'

'My dear Hans, you must be sick. Where do you get these notions from? It's absolutely ludicrous . . . And, in any case, how could you possibly be "brought down"?'

'Now you'd really like to know that, wouldn't you? I warn you,

Pétur – you know as well as I do that you can't touch me. You'll simply end by putting yourself in court. Don't do it!'

Pétur's face had gone pale. But he said nothing; and a moment later, the two men were riding at speed along the Lagarfljót, silent and set in their angers.

*　　*　　*

May 24th 1748

There was a moment on the way to court yesterday when I had a mind just to cut him down there and then. Dear God, I must try and be more careful or I'll ruin everything. After all, to kill him would be nothing: he must fall and be seen to fall – his family's name must lie in the muck where it belongs.

Eight years now since this was entrusted to me. How much longer? Father gives me no peace. The whole time now my head's full of the noise – and right inside it, part of it, his voice, going on and on. Why isn't it done? Have I forgotten? Why won't I let him rest?

How has HW suddenly seen what I'm after? Anyway, now it needs to be done soon, if I'm to keep my name clean. It's Sigurdur that's the problem. When I tried to push him, he turned on me, the tyke. Told me to leave him be. Said he knew things about father. Said maybe I should make it worth his while, if I wanted the case seen through. I just laughed at him. But that was three years ago. And now, even though I started making him small payments last winter, he's still done precious little.

But my letter to Jón will have done the trick. He still believes I'm his only hope. Lord Jesus, may it please You to see fit to let justice come about soon!

*　　*　　*

Hjardarhlíd, Fljótsdalur
May 24th 1748

Dear Governor,
May I make so bold as to bring to your notice the fact that Sunnefa Jónsdóttir and her brother Jón have now been detained in custody for some four and a half years since they appeared at the Great Assembly in 1743? I fully realize that my own supposed implication in this case makes any intervention on my part suspect and that consequently you may find it hard to believe that I am not, in fact, writing this letter

128

motivated by a desire to protect myself. This conclusion, I fear, may be inevitable: but I can assure you that I am so certain of my innocence that, by pressing for justice to be swiftly administered in the case, I have no fears whatsoever of endangering my own future.

The main purpose of this letter is, however, to lodge an official objection to Pétur Thorsteinsson as the head of the investigation of the case. As a sheriff here in Múlasýsla and therefore my colleague, he has, I think, been put in a very unfair situation by this appointment; and I firmly believe that the case would be more rapidly concluded if he were to be withdrawn and a substitute found. I think it is also not out of place to mention here that there have been some minor differences of opinion between myself and Pétur Thorsteinsson in the past and that consequently it would be impossible for him to take a wholly objective attitude to his work in this matter. But may I once again stress that I inform you of this not in any way for personal reasons but purely so that the chances of justice being perverted may be minimized?

Hans Wium
Sheriff

       ★   ★   ★

Sigurdur Stefánsson looked up in surprise at the man standing in the doorway; but before addressing him, he automatically leant down and turned the key in the lock of the big chest by his side. He slipped the key into his pocket and, with a bleak smile, spoke.

'Yes?'

The man made no movement and his face was a match for Sigurdur's in coldness. The eyes were still and dead, the mouth no more than a cut in the heavily pocked face, where a blunt nose did little to relieve the massiveness of the features. One nostril had been damaged and there were only odd tufts of hair on his white, scaly head. He stood like a stack of granite, his hands hanging by his sides, and stared down at the diminutive sheriff.

'Well – what do you want?' asked Sigurdur brusquely. 'I don't know you, do I?'

The man said nothing but reached inside his jacket and took out two letters. Both were sealed – one with blue, the other with red wax. He looked at them carefully and then held out one of them, pointing at the name written on it. He seemed unaware that he was

129

holding it upside down, but when the sheriff tried to take the letter to turn it round, the man seized his wrist so fiercely that Sigurdur all but cried out in pain. Craning round to read the writing, he saw that the letter was addressed to Jón Jónsson. Sigurdur looked up and spoke slowly, now realizing that the man was most probably both deaf and dumb. And indeed when he explained that Jón was through in the byre shoeing the horses, he noticed the man watching his lips. Sigurdur then asked whom the other letter was for. Still with a completely expressionless face, the man gave it to him and stepped back again. Casting a nervous glance up at his visitor, Sigurdur broke the seal.

Dear Sigurdur,

I am sending by the same messenger who bears this note, a letter for Jón Jónsson. I have seen my way to helping you out but as you still consistently refuse to do the work expected of you in the case concerning Hans Wium, I am now following up certain possibilities myself. It may well be that when Jón reads the letter, he will decide that he wishes to make a formal statement with regard to the case. If this is so, please let me know immediately so that I can take the necessary action. The messenger has been instructed to bring back both your answer and the letter to Jón when the boy has read it. I trust that you will be discreet.

P

Sigurdur read the note through again and frowned.

'Do you know Jón Jónsson?'

The man moved his head slowly from side to side.

'Right,' said Sigurdur getting up.

They went out and made their way along the front of the buildings. Sigurdur opened the byre door and called out in a shrill voice.

'Jón! Jón! Are you there, boy?'

From behind a horse, the young man stood up. Soon to be twenty-three, Jón had filled out into a powerful young man, tall and broad. He made no answer to the sheriff but stood there holding the hammer and eyeing the newcomer who stood by the door.

'You read well enough, don't you, lad? There's a letter come for you.'

Sigurdur turned to take the letter from the man but once more found himself faced by the same unblinking gaze. The man made a blunt gesture towards the door, telling him to leave. Deciding not to insist, the little man left with as much of a show of disdain as his game leg would allow.

Sigurdur's family at Smyrlabjörg consisted of his large wife, Rannveig, and a daughter called Thórdís, a slow, heavily-built girl with a round, flat face and curly brown hair. His three sons had long since left the district, unable to stomach their father's meanness and sour temper. For tight-fisted greed was what drove Sigurdur Stefánsson, a greed that knew neither scruple nor limit; and it was this greed that made both his farm such a run-down place and himself so disliked by all. He had been good at satisfying this greed, good at loans and timely foreclosures, at buying from the desperate and selling to the needy, at pressing the obstinate just before hearing a case of theirs in the court – and so steadily filling the old Danish sea-chest that he kept bolted to the floor at Smyrlabjörg.

His appointment as counsel for the prosecution in the case of Sunnefa and Hans Wium came about because Joakim Lafrentz, laid up in bed at the time of the Assembly, had been maliciously advised by a man who had been worsted by Sigurdur in a business deal. It was well known that to be delegated to a lawsuit brought a great deal of work with little or no recompense – which seemed a discreet but particularly fitting revenge to take on Sigurdur.

Although Sigurdur had been indignant and angry at the announcement, once back in Sudursveit, far from both Thingvellir and Reykjavík, he soon returned to his slothful ways and put all thought of the case out of his mind, believing that it would be a long time before anyone bothered him about it. What did he care about some half-Danish fool of a sheriff who'd gone and got himself embroiled with a vicious country girl?

But he was mistaken in thinking himself safe for, almost immediately, he received a letter from Lafrentz, reminding him that the whole matter was to be sorted out as soon as possible and urging him to begin work without delay. Sigurdur had left the letter unanswered for a while and had then written back saying that he was unable to initiate the enquiry since Hans Wium had not yet paid him the ten rix-dollars that were to cover his costs. For some months he heard no more . . .

One morning in the week before the Christmas of 1743, he had sat at his desk with both hands resting on the pommel of his stick and peered down his nose at the letter which had just arrived from

Höfn. His lips were pursed and his forehead wrinkled as he read the letter with an air of bored condescension.

Reykjavík, December 11th 1743

Dear Sheriff,

I am afraid that my recent indisposition has prevented me from answering your letter of September last until now.

I see from your letter that Sheriff Wium has not yet paid you the ten rix-dollars that the Great Assembly imposed on him as a fine. This may well be, but I cannot impress on you too strongly how important it is that this case concerning Sheriff Wium and the girl Sunnefa Jónsdóttir should be concluded at the earliest possible date. Consequently, it is quite unacceptable to me that you should use the non-payment of this sum to excuse yourself for not collecting the necessary information to support your prosecution. Five months have now elapsed since your appointment to the case; and since this period of time has seen so little progress in your investigations, I must now insist that you take immediate steps to complete the preparation of the prosecution.

I enclose ten rix-dollars from my own personal budget and trust that you will understand by this irregular payment how concerned I am that the unfortunate business should not get protracted one day longer than is necessary.

I shall be writing to Henrik Ochsen, the Minister for the Colonies in Copenhagen, at Easter and, by that time, I shall expect to be able to give him some information on the progress of the case as he has already expressed to me his extreme dissatisfaction over the whole matter.

Joakim Hendriksen Lafrentz
Governor

'. . . his extreme dissatisfaction over the whole matter,' Sigurdur had repeated, displaying his yellow teeth as he mimicked the letter in front of him. 'What's it to me what some pompous fool in Copenhagen thinks? And anyway, that Lafrentz will be lucky if he's still with us by Easter . . . Pah!' he had said, pushing the letter aside. But then he had broken into a smile as he touched the little bag of money that had come in the same package.

Sigurdur wrote the governor a long and obsequious letter. Then, only a month or so later, he heard of Lafrentz's collapse and once again thought himself free. But he was soon receiving regular letters from Pétur Thorsteinsson, at first full of helpful suggestions and then, as time passed, with a growing number of complaints. From the tone of these letters, he quickly deduced that Pétur had some interest in the case that was more than professional – and from that moment had no trouble in holding him off, with a mixture of prevarication and pretence. He was also not long in discovering quite another reason for holding back on the case, for Jón proved himself to be a worker quite unlike any that Sigurdur had had at Smyrlabjörg before. Jón himself, wretched and lonely, knew of no other way to deaden the tedium of his life and so worked himself to exhaustion.

When Sigurdur's party left Thingvellir that bright, windy day, they had just crossed the great river, Thjórsá, when somebody tapped Jón on the shoulder and pointed out Angantýr Atlason's farm of Glúmsstadir, where Sunnefa was to be held. But it had been another four days' journey on from there, a long, complicated route behind the glaciers before they crossed the dark wastes of Skeidarár-sandur that lay to the west of Sudursveit. Five years later, when he had almost given up all hope, his boyhood was quite behind him, a change that had come about in the silence of solitude and separation from the one thing he loved.

In the afternoon of the day on which the man came to Smyrlabjörg with the two letters, Jón was nowhere to be seen.

'Where have you been?' said Sigurdur when Jón finally came into the kitchen.

Jón pointed northwards with his thumb. There was anger in his eyes as he helped himself to food from the stove.

'Where?'

'Up on the glacier.'

'Whatever for?'

'If you really want to know, I was just trying out some crampons I made during the winter.'

'And what about the horses? I don't suppose you finished them, did you?'

'No – but they'll get done, right enough.'

'Now look, lad – you're not here on holiday, you know. We can't afford to keep you if you're just going to go running about amusing yourself like this. The roof will need to . . .'

'Do your own bloody roof, you little tightwad! And don't you try telling me how to work – I get more done in a week than everybody else put together would do in a century. So just stop your yapping and give me some peace, will you?'

In all the time that he had been at Smyrlabjörg, nobody had ever seen Jón like this before. They were used to him silent and impassive; so that this sudden show of anger quite puzzled them. While they all sat about discussing it in low voices, Jón finished his bowl of broth and walked out.

Though it still blew vigorously, the wind had slackened since the afternoon. Out beyond the long sand-bar, the sea was all muddiness and foam: on the land, where there was neither bush nor tree to feel the wind, it was like a booming stillness, without sign of life.

Jón walked slowly away from the farm, his head sunk. When he had come to the edge of the sands, where a river forked out for the sea, he sat down in the shelter of a boulder and stared with heavy eyes into the thundering twilight before him.

When he at last got back, Sigurdur looked up at him.

'The man's staying the night,' he said. 'He'll need to bed down with you.'

An hour or so later, when everyone was asleep, the messenger was startled awake by a blade pricking against his throat. Opening his eyes, he saw by the weak light the young man staring at him and gesturing towards the stairs.

Their movements masked by the wind, the two men padded downstairs. Once below, Jón stopped him by the window.

'Do you know the way west?'

The man nodded.

Later, the two shadowy figures made their way over to the byre. They saddled a couple of the best horses and roped up two others as spares. Leading them away from the building, they rode off down the coast with Jón beside, but just behind, his guide.

*   *   *

Dear Jón (the letter had read)

It is my unhappy duty to inform you that your sister, Sunnefa, is dead. Unfortunately I must also tell you that I have reason to believe that she was murdered. I believe that her death was brought about by poison and that the person on whose instructions the poison was administered was none other than Hans Wium. I think that once you hear this terrible news, you will no longer have any hesitation about

giving evidence that you were a witness to Sheriff Wium's assault on
your poor sister at Axlir in 1741. If this is so, you have only to tell
Sigurdur Stefánsson that you wish to make a formal statement and he
will let me know immediately. This letter is to be returned to me via
the messenger who brought it. I send you my sincere condolences on
this sad event and ask for your full co-operation in bringing to justice
the instigator of these crimes.

Pétur Thorsteinsson

★   ★   ★

Urged on by Jón, they rode hard through the spring night and were already clear of the parish by the time the light came up. All that day, they pressed on; and it was not until they reached the edge of the great sands that they finally stopped to rest. But by noon the following day, they had taken the horses across the edge of the glacier and were once again moving west at speed.

From the beginning, Jón had sensed the man's watchfulness and so had kept himself constantly on guard against any surprise. But then, one evening when they were crossing a steep slope out to the north of the glaciers, there came a moment when the man suddenly found himself directly above Jón; and with no more than a grunt of exertion, he turned and hurled himself down at him. Such was the force of his attack that both men and two of the horses were sent tumbling down the scree in a cloud of dust. The horses, tied together and sliding out of control, struck a rock and vanished over a cliff. Jón, coming to rest just higher up, turned to see the man leaping down on him. Twisting clear of the attack, he heard little more than a skittering of loose stones as the man went past and on over the edge. Peering down, Jón could see no sign of him; but, waiting no longer, he quickly caught the other horses and rode off, glad to be free and now sure that he could find his way through.

When the best of the light had gone, Jón pitched camp and bedded down. It was in the early hours that he surfaced abruptly from a dream and lay half-awake, hearing the horses moving restlessly behind him. But it was a shuffling sound closer by that fully woke him and sent him turning for his knife. There in the pale, hazy light, he saw the man, cut about and bloody, with one arm hanging uselessly, stumbling towards him with a rock aimed at his head.

The blow caught Jón heavily on the shoulder. And in the next instant, with the full weight of the man on top of him, he felt teeth trying to get in at his throat. Scarcely able to move, Jón felt for the man's eyes and tore; and as the teeth released him, he brought the heavy knife up and drove it into the man's side.

For two further days, Jón rode slowly on through the hills with a growing fever, knowing only that he had to reach Angantýr's farm. Cloud and drizzle came in for a time; but when at last they peeled back, he turned south-west by the sun and soon after entered the district of Land. Later that same day, he came riding up the slope to the sheriff's farm and struck the door.

Some old women took him in and cleaned him up. A broken collar-bone, they said and told him to lie still. But Sunnefa? he heard himself asking. And they would nod and smile . . .

He awoke to a noise of voices, men talking loudly over the shrill protestations of the old women. The door pushed open and a thick-set man came in.

'Come on, lad,' he said, 'get yourself dressed. You're coming back with us.'

There were four of them, sent up from Sudursveit, pressed into service and by now short-tempered and bent on getting back as soon as possible.

'You'll need to wait and see what Angantýr says,' insisted one of the women. 'He'll know what to do. They should all be back by tonight.'

'You can't let him ride like that,' said another. 'The bone's not set.'

'Strap him up and get us some food,' answered the man. 'We'll be leaving straightaway.'

The old woman helping Jón dress munched her gums thoughtfully and then leaned forward.

'She's up at the shieling, lad. Don't you go worrying – she's fit and well.'

They left soon afterwards, Jón sitting upright, looking almost carefree.

Sunnefa was alive!

*   *   *

It was another May, two years later.

That evening, up by the Lagarfljót, the weather was wet and

windless as Einar rode back along the track. The spare horse, with which he had set out from Hjardarhlíd earlier in the day, now carried a middle-aged woman called Ingunn, who was generally considered to be the best midwife in the area. After all those years of seeming barrenness, Gudrún was about to give birth to her first child.

Through the months of Gudrún's pregnancy, the house at Hjardarhlíd had once again been filled with cheerfulness. Having had his application for Pétur's replacement turned down by the governor, Hans appeared to have put the whole matter out of his mind and once more to be fully taken up with his work. When, in that autumn of 1749, it was heard that he was looking forward to being a father, people were sure that at last Hans's life had taken a real turn for the better.

Yet privately, Hans was not wholly at peace. Still the thought of the two being held dogged him through the days and the long waking moments of the nights. Yet, as ever, on this matter he felt himself pinned, forced to remain inactive, aware that every word he spoke on it could only invite the reawakening of buried suspicions. In the secrecy of his thoughts though, there was all the revolt of indignation against the iron resolve of the law. Had the two of them not paid their dues by the seven years of their confinement? But the law, it would seem, was the law . . . And then Hans's anger would boil over on to Pétur, the one man who had the power to save and spare them.

But for the moment at least, Hans's thoughts were completely elsewhere. A few hours after Ingunn the midwife arrived at Hjardarhlíd, Hans's son was born. Six days later, three weeks before midsummer, in hot, calm weather, Nikulás the minister christened the child Niels Kristján Wium; and, afterwards, a great feast of roast lamb and ale was given in front of the farmhouse, lasting far into the night.

It would have seemed that the birth of their son marked not only a turning-point in Hans and Gudrún's marriage but also an end to the years of sadness and unease that had followed Sunnefa's trial at Thingvellir.

*   *   *   .

'Hans! Hans!'

Einar's voice rang with urgency as he hurried down the corridor and burst into the room where Hans and Gudrún were sitting playing with Niels.

'Hans, it's come!' he said, holding up a letter.

For a moment, Hans's expression changed. The smiling flicker of his eyes was arrested; the shape of his mouth, open in pleasure, hardened. Then, once again, he relaxed and laughed.

'My dear Einar! You come charging in like some grey-haired prophet of doom, frightening the wits out of all of us. Come along, we'll go into the study and have a look at this letter of yours.'

'Well, Einar, it's happened at last, has it?' he said as he closed the door.

The secretary nodded and handed Hans the letter.

'Please say nothing about this to Gudrún,' said Hans grimly when he had read it through. 'As you know, she's not been well lately.'

'But Hans, that's all very well but you won't be able to keep it from her for long. Your replacement, Jón Sigurdsson, is to take over at the end of the month. Then what'll you do?'

'I haven't decided yet,' replied Hans pensively. 'I think my only hope lies in my getting to Denmark. As far as I can make out, none of this would ever have come about if it hadn't been for Rantzau, the new minister in Copenhagen. If what you told me is right, almost the first thing he did when he took up office last year was to write to Pingel, telling him to get the case sorted out immediately. Well, I don't suppose he realized just how optimistic he was being. As it is, it's taken him the best part of nine months to organize it all. Anyway, Pingel obviously didn't want to get involved and so simply instructed Pétur to stop delaying the case. As a start, he'll have told him to carry out one of Rantzau's main recommendations, namely that I should be suspended. Pétur must've been only too delighted. No, there's no doubt about it – it all came from Rantzau. I've somehow got to get to see him.'

'But what happens when Jón Sigurdsson arrives?'

'I'll take Gudrún and Niels to Höskuldsstadasel,' said Hans firmly. 'I'm afraid you'll have to stay here, Einar. Don't worry – I mean to get my job back. But in the meantime it'll be much better for you to stay and act as Jón's secretary. He's not a bad man . . . But, as I say, please keep quiet about it all for the moment.'

*　　*　　*

138

Gudjón Pálsson, for all his weight and cumbersome build, rode his horse with surprising verve. His wattled cheeks juddered lightly from the rhythms of the horse's fast trotting as he climbed from the valley behind him. The April sunshine, falling out of a windy blue sky, touched him with a warmth that was a joy after the fiery cold of the early morning.

He had left Hvannabrekka at daybreak with three of Pétur's best horses and instructions that he was to spare no effort in getting over to Fáskrúdsjördur by mid-afternoon. Pétur had heard that a boat, bound for Århus in Denmark, was leaving the fjord that evening and that Hans Wium was planning to be on it. He had quickly drawn up a warrant stopping him from leaving the country until the case concerning him had been dealt with. It was this that Gudjón carried as he rode up towards the head of the valley.

Now forty-five, Gudjón's thickened features gave him a look of coarseness and cold cunning. Many years before, it had been a theft allowed to pass without prosecution that had been the beginning of his obligation to Pétur; and this had steadily become compounded by a list of small crimes that now made for quite a bond, of criminality and connivance, between the sheriff and his farmhand.

As regards Pétur himself, Gudjón no longer knew quite what to think. For though Pétur still gave all the appearances of normality in public, with a clear intelligence and shrewdness of judgement, the ten years since the trial at Thingvellir had seen a gradual increase in the peculiarity of his private behaviour. More and more often now, Gudjón heard him talking to himself late at night, saw him pacing up and down shaking his head, stopping and staring at the ground, striking his thigh angrily, then walking on, shaking his head once more. Even the others at Hvannabrekka noticed how when you were talking to him, his eyes would suddenly leave you, just as if his attention had been caught by somebody else.

For another five miles, the man and his small horses thrust on up through the snow, with the range of ice-covered ridges above and the dazzling cut of the wind falling out of a polished sky. But at last, passing over the top through billowing turmoils of powder snow, he saw far below him the darker colours of bare ground and, beyond that, tucked in at the head of the fjord, the boat riding at anchor. With an eye on the sun, he changed horses and hurried on.

An hour later, he reached the shore and quickly found a man to row him out to the merchantman. He had just climbed aboard and was talking to the captain when the door to the companion-way opened and Hans appeared.

'Gudjón! What brings you down here then?'

'You can forget about sailing for the moment, Sheriff Wium. I've got a warrant here.'

'A warrant? Let me see.'

Hans had changed greatly in the two years that he had been at Höskuldsstadasel. Although only thirty-eight, his thick brown hair was stranded with grey. The sockets of his eyes looked darkened and his cheeks, formerly rounded, were now flatter, with the skin drawn tight over the cheek-bones. But it was the little pucker above his nose that seemed to show the weariness and misery which had come with the months of his disgrace.

'God in heaven!' he said under his breath as he read the document. 'Can't they let me be for once?'

He looked up and stared out to sea. At length, he blinked and turned to the captain with a characteristic show of light-heartedness.

'Well, Captain Eriksen, it seems that I shan't be sailing with you today after all. I'm sorry to have troubled you. Will this do to cover the cost of the inconvenience I've caused you?' he said, reaching into his pocket.

The old sailor looked at the money and shrugged.

When they were back on land, Hans turned to Gudjón.

'You can wipe that smile off your fat face, you hireling!' he said. 'And tell that man at Hvannabrekka I'm not finished yet.'

'Who do you think you're fooling?' answered Gudjón. 'You were finished years ago.'

*   *   *

December 29th 1753
Pressure, always more pressure. He must succumb. And then I shall sleep. Blessed Lord, I am Your servant, I am Your branding angel. I bear Your fire into the darkest corners of our world, I light up the horrors of the darkness.

*   *   *

'It will not do!' cried Pétur, gripping the edge of the table. 'It just will not do! This is the third court I have summoned him to appear before. The man flouts me, he flouts our country's laws! It will not do, I say!'

The other members of the court, local officials, looked down in embarrassment. They all knew that what he said was true but this fevered outburst left them stunned and dimly conscious that they were witnessing something more than a judicial denouncement of Hans's absence.

'Perhaps we could suggest to him . . .' one of them started to say.

'We'll suggest nothing! I tell you we'll order him to appear! We'll threaten him with indictment at the Great Assembly! We'll . . . we'll . . .' he spluttered. 'It's outrageous!'

★ ★ ★

I never thought we would manage it.

It was fairly clear that Eiríkur was one of the few people who might be able to secure permission for Hans to go to Denmark; but the great question was whether we could find a way of circumventing his naively rigid moral attitude to the whole thing. Eiríkur, like the rest of us, knew that although Hans was innocent, he would have little chance of clearing himself unless he got to Copenhagen. And yet he seemed unable to reconcile the logical conclusion to this, which was that some false excuse must be produced to get him out of the country.

I tried speaking to Gudný about this.

'But Einar,' she said, 'you've absolutely no idea of how it's all a matter of black and white for Eiríkur. And there's no way of twisting his ideas by argument. So if you want him to do anything about this, you'll have to deceive him. Just don't ask me to help you, that's all.'

Well, I thought to myself, if there's to be any deception, the fewer people who are involved, or who even know of it, the better. I went back to Hjardarhlíd and put my mind to the problem.

A week later, I rode over to Höskuldsstadasel and handed Hans a letter, telling him that it had arrived at Hjardarhlíd a few days before.

'Good Lord!' he exclaimed on opening it. 'It's from some man in Denmark about my aunt, Irmelin. Do you remember, Gudrún? I stayed with her and my uncle, Frederik Børge, when I was at uni-

141

versity. She must be nearly eighty now . . . The letter says that she keeps asking if I can find the time to come and sort out her husband's estate. Apparently, the two sons have all but been at blows since their father's death – and she doesn't feel she can trust anybody else.'

'Hans, you must go,' said Gudrún quickly, in a determined voice.

'It's no good just telling me that I must go . . . you know very well that I can't.'

'But surely, Hans,' put in Gudný, 'in the circumstances, you could ask for permission to be away for a while, couldn't you? It'd be inhuman to refuse you.'

'Well, perhaps . . . though I'd have to be away for some time,' said Hans. 'But how do you suggest I get permission?'

'What about Eiríkur?' I interjected.

Four weeks later, early in September 1754, I rode with Hans over to Seydisfjördur from where a fast boat was about to leave for Denmark. Eiríkur, genuinely touched by the story of Hans's aunt, had used Pétur's temporary absence at the Great Assembly to apply to a sheriff in Nordur-Thingeyjarsýsla for the necessary document to release Hans; and had come back with permission for Hans to be out of the country for a maximum of eighteen months. Should Hans stay away longer, he would automatically incur not only a heavy fine but also serious prejudice against himself in the case.

Our journey went off uneventfully; and when we finally found ourselves in Seydisfjördur, waiting for a boat to take us out to the ship, I turned to Hans and delivered the little speech I had prepared.

'Well, Hans, now that you're on your way and we shan't be seeing you for a while, I've a little favour to ask of you.'

'But of course, my friend. And what's that?' said Hans with a smile.

'Well, I want you to take this letter and to promise not to read it until you're at sea.'

He took the letter and looked at me with a mixture of warmth and suspicion.

'This is all very mysterious, Einar. But it doesn't seem much to ask.'

A few minutes later, I was standing by myself on the shore, watching the open boat pulling away over the water to the three-master. She was due to sail in two hours.

*　　*　　*

Dear Hans,

It's more than probable that you'll never quite trust me again after you've read this letter. But, for my own pride at least, it's important that you understand that what I've done, I've done purely in the hope that it'd help you.

The letter which I brought you from your aunt was a forgery. Your aunt, so far as I know, is well and has no greater concerns about the estate than she had before. But as I hope you'll now see, the only way in which I could hope to persuade you and, indirectly, Eiríkur of an urgent reason for your going to Denmark was to make none of you partner to my lies. I recalled your having received a letter a while back from your aunt and, having found it among your papers, set about concocting a suitable forgery from various facts concerning the estate to which your aunt had referred.

May you have every success in your difficult mission and return to us soon to take up your rightful job once more.

Your humble and half-
repentant secretary,
Einar

Hans looked up from the letter and stared back across the bubbling wake to the skyline of mountain-tops which was all that remained in sight as the boat ran south-eastwards before a bounding wind. For a while, he was lost in thought; and then his face broke open into a broad smile.

'Einar Eyjólfsson!' he said, laughing aloud and smacking the wooden rail with the flat of his hand. 'A man of hidden talents!'

*   *   *

Soon after Hans had sailed, the summer's last days came in, with their sheaves of thick light and with sudden, portentous evenings of smoky air and new chill. The skeins of geese, passing over high in the pale skies for the ocean crossing, had soon gone; and already the sun, even at midday, was a lessened force, a mere brightness arcing low over the hills.

All that autumn and winter, the volcano, Katla, was in full erup-tion down in the south of the country; in Fljótsdalur, however, once Pétur had got over his rage at Hans's escape, everything was quiet.

143

Now Pétur could only retire to his study at Hvannabrekka and brood on what might have been – and on what might somehow still come to be. He saw Hans in Copenhagen, a half-Dane among Danes, using his eloquence to get himself reinstated by the Supreme Court. And so he began to make his plans accordingly.

In the early days, he had been content to let the case not come to trial: rumour and hearsay had been more efficient, working like the mouldering of mildew on Hans's name. But once the tide of opinion had turned, only a reopening of the case, with new evidence, was going to be sufficient. He had often thought of forcing Hans or Sunnefa to make a statement under oath; but had always feared that the earlier incest and the subsequent meeting of Sunnefa and her brother at the bothy might confuse the issue. He now decided that to settle it once and for all, he would somehow bring the case to trial again – and produce a new witness, Gudjón, who would testify that he had actually seen the assault take place.

While Pétur thus began to feel a new optimism, and everyone at Höskuldsstadasel was being cheered by the letters arriving from Hans in Denmark, Sunnefa herself, at Glúmsstadir, had fallen into a decline. In recent months, she had begun talking about her two children, the children she had scarcely known, how she had brought them into this world only to abandon them, how she had been nothing of a mother to them, how there was only badness in her, badness and more badness and all the shame . . . And the people of Glúmsstadir, seeing that the obsession was turning her mind, sent word to the doctor, Gunnar Thórdarson, who was newly arrived from Copenhagen, asking that he should come and look at her the next time he was passing.

In the event, however, Gunnar was so taken up with the general state of ill-health throughout the south that he only reached Land the following spring, by which time Sunnefa's mind had collapsed. She seemed not to hear what the doctor had to say to her, seemed to be quite closed off and unreachable. She sat there, endlessly pressing her finger-tips together, and only once spoke, when she suddenly interrupted him and said:

'But why had he taken off his silver ring?'

Before riding off, all Gunnar could do was to suggest a light diet and plenty of exercise, though he knew that, as things stood, she would almost certainly slip into further seclusion before the onset of dementia.

Towards the end of the second winter following Hans's departure, Pétur began to anticipate the possibility of Hans failing to return within the allocated time. He saw this as an ideal platform from which to launch his new attack, by turning the people once more against Hans, even before he was brought to court. But before he could begin to spread this feeling, a letter arrived from a judge of the Supreme Court, officially giving Hans leave to be away for a further five months.

At Höskuldsstadasel, they had been receiving regular letters from Hans. These were full of hope but asked them to be patient as there was no way of getting his case quickly before the overburdened courts. The matter of an obscure sheriff out in the colonies would, no doubt, eventually get heard; but it was clearly unlikely to take priority.

The spring and then the summer passed much as in the previous few years, grey-skied and rainless, so that when harvest-time came, late in July, there was a pitiful supply of grass to be cut for winter fodder. As usual, once the harvest was over, the district officers informed Pétur and Jón Sigurdsson, and a notice was posted at the church, telling everyone when and where to meet for the autumn round-up of the sheep. That year the meeting was to be held on the Tuesday of the third week in August, at the farm of Birkihlíd up at the northern end of the Lagarfljót.

That August Tuesday was a day typical of the recent summers. A grey, featureless sky hung low, while a cold north-easterly wind sliced down off the hills and tore up confusions of dust from the dry ground. In the early part of the morning, the men began to ride in from all directions; and by midday eighty or ninety of them, with almost twice as many horses, had gathered at Birkihlíd. As they stood about talking, the noise was like that of light surf, broken here and there by shouts and laughter and the whinnying of horses. The smells in the air were those of leather and rancid mutton fat, of sweat and dung, and of the great broth which was being prepared in the farm. Every farm in the district had, by custom, sent at least one man to take part and they formed a rough collection as they stood and exchanged news and sniffed at the air in anticipation of the food.

There were men with smooth, polished faces; there were massive men, bearded, with raucous, toothless laughs; there were wiry, taut-bodied men, with faces covered with stubble, raw from decades of wind and sleet – men young and old but held by the common bond of hunger. A lethargy of eyes, shadowed cheeks, the hollow racking of coughs – the signs of it were everywhere, and they knew they had only hope and prayer to fall back on.

Eventually, one of the farmers clambered on to a rock and held up his hands for silence.

'Friends!' he cried. 'Listen! We'll take the route we took the year before last. We'll start off up the back here and go north till we're out on Bótarheidi. Then we'll come west and do the slopes as far as the beginning of Jökuldalur. After that, we'll need to . . .'

His voice slowed and faded away as he stared out over the crowd to the hillside beyond. People turned to follow his gaze.

Down across the slope rode a large man with three pack horses. He was moving fast and the tail of his green coat was lifted by the wind. As he caught sight of the crowd, he pulled in his horses and stopped, raising his hand high in greeting.

'Hans!' somebody cried. 'It's Hans!'

And immediately the cry was taken up. As the rider brought his horses down off the hill towards the farm, he was met by barrages of sound from the farmers. Again and again they called his name and then took up the rhythm, beating with the flats of their hands on their saddles.

When Hans had ridden up to the rock, one of the farmers called out to him.

'What news then, Hans?'

'Good news, my friends!' he said expansively.

'What news?' they all cried.

'News of a holiday for Jón Sigurdsson!' he laughed. 'The poor man longs for his home lands in Tungusveit. Let him go! He's done his duty! I'm sheriff in Fljótsdalur now!'

A roar burst up from the men. And as Hans stood there with open arms, the slapping of saddles was taken up again and rose into a wild ovation.

*   *   *

That autumn, there was much talk of a trial.

The Supreme Court had reinstated Hans on the strict understanding that, as soon as possible after his return, a court was to be convened and the various witnesses summoned. This court was to be held by Jón Sigurdsson; and both Sunnefa and Jón, as well as

146

Hans, were to be present to give evidence as required. The court was not to be dissolved until a final verdict had been reached and this verdict, in its turn, was to be put before the Great Assembly for confirmation the following summer. If the Supreme Court saw that the annals of the Great Assembly for 1757 did not record the case as being concluded, it would not only suspend Hans once more but also ban him from office for life. Hans had eleven months in which to clear himself.

It had just been agreed to hold the court in the last week of October when a spell of bad weather brought blizzards that closed the passes and cut off Fljótsdalur from the rest of the country. And so it continued all winter, the weather wild and cheerless, with heavy falls of snow and numerous avalanches, and it soon became clear that the trial would now have to be held over until the spring.

Pétur, snowed in at Hvannabrekka, was quite calm. He was now sure that, whatever happened, the trial would at last take place; and that once Sunnefa had been prompted to call on Gudjón as a witness, nothing further could go wrong. At Hjardarhlíd, after the high spirits surrounding Hans's return, the postponement did little to ease the anxiety over the Supreme Court's stipulations. Seeking to distract himself, Hans turned more and more to his son, now six years old, who had grown into a beautiful if rather frail child, with his mother's fair hair and grey eyes. Maybe Hans would have wished a ruder health for his boy, but otherwise he saw only the perfection of those innocent years shining in him. It was perhaps this very innocence that held Hans so engrossed, that he sought as a counter to all that seemed so sullied and rotten in his own life. But while it touched Gudrún to find Hans and Niels totally absorbed in some game or story, she also knew her man well enough to know that this was partly just another refusal to face the coming problems of the spring.

It was after the celebrations on Christmas Eve, when they were sitting late by the fire, that Gudrún touched once more on the old subject.

'You haven't come to a decision yet, have you? You know – about what you'll say to them in the spring.'

'Gudrún, what's there to decide? We've been over it all a thousand times. Look, if I admit that I was up there that day, the only thing that'll persuade a court of my innocence is if I state, on oath, that I never touched the girl. As I've always maintained, all that happened

147

was that I went into the bothy, told the girl to get dressed and then went outside to wait for her. After that, I just don't know. If I couldn't remember fifteen years ago, I certainly can't remember now.'

'But Hans, for God's sake, you'll . . . it'll be the ruin of us, it will! It's not just me – think of Niels, for pity's sake!'

'Nothing will happen to Niels, I swear. You know that. But it's no good – I still can't, won't, take an oath when I'm not sure of the truth. You must see that!'

'But Hans – be reasonable!'

A silence fell between them. A drop of moisture hissed in the embers. The wind whined over the snow-bound roof.

'It's the word of that girl, that wretched misled girl, that's going to bring me down,' said Hans darkly a while later. 'Without that, there'd be no case.'

His voice tailed off as he relapsed into thought. Gudrún sniffed miserably.

'God damn her!' she hissed.

'No, Gudrún – God knows, the fault's not hers. If you feel anger, keep it for another.'

'Oh, I suppose you mean Pétur,' said Gudrún sharply. 'Well, perhaps you're right but I'd as soon strangle that nasty little bitch and kill the lie at source!'

When, in the middle of April, the spring came, it came dramatically. Almost overnight, the hard frost receded and the soft winds and rains blew up over the hills to bring back life to the countryside, long paralysed by the ice and snow. Day after day, the rains fell and the level of water in the rivers and lakes started to rise. Whole hillsides, which normally carried a handful of small streams, now poured with water. Even the track that passed along the Lagarfljót soon became a morass where horses would sink up to their chests and flounder till pulled clear with ropes. And so it was that, after waiting patiently for the cold and darkness to pass, the people now found themselves standing in their doorways, watching the torrents of rain and wondering how long it would be before they could get through to the fjords in the east for supplies.

In the autumn, it had been left that as soon as the weather permitted, somebody was to be sent south to collect Sunnefa and Jón, while a message was to go north to Jón Sigurdsson, informing him of the date set for the trial. A man from one of the farms near

Hjardarhlíd was told to prepare to go north; the man chosen to fetch the two prisoners was Gudjón Pálsson. As the rain continued to pour down, both men stood by and everybody watched the level of the rivers. Slowly the days passed by.

★   ★   ★

There was a man called Thórarinn Bragason who lived at Svartagil in Nordurdalur. He was a slovenly creature whose farm was a disgrace to the neighbourhood. Leases of farms were held indefinitely unless the tenant was guilty of some serious crime or if he could be seen to be neglecting the property. For the latter reason and after many warnings, Pétur had recently discontinued Thórarinn's lease at Svartagil and had told him that he would have to find himself a place in some other part of the county. Because of this, it was common knowledge in the district that Thórarinn would have liked a chance of getting his own back on the sheriff.

The spring thaw came to an end as suddenly as it had started. The weather grew steadily warmer and the sun shone in a calm sky. Less than a week later, on the last day of April, the ford became passable and messages were exchanged between Hjardarhlíd and Hvannabrekka fixing the date of the trial. It was set for May 23rd; and, only hours later, the two men set off on their respective journeys.

The following day, Gudrún was sitting by the window, sewing. Her eyes were red and she stared at her work without really seeing it. Now that the trial was so imminent, she knew that she had to try and do something, since Hans so steadfastly refused to help himself. But what? If she had been crying earlier, it was not from any misery or self-pity but purely out of frustration. Something, she must think of something . . .

A while later, Thórarinn Bragason rode up from the ford. He raised his hand to her as he passed and then went into the farmhouse. When he came out, he rode off along the Lagarfljót and, rounding a knoll, found himself face to face with Gudrún. She was finely dressed and rode sidesaddle on a young horse.

'Hello, Thórarinn. Better weather at last.'

'Yes, thank God.'

'How's Pétur Thorsteinsson these days?'

149

'That's hardly a fair question to ask me – you're the wife of a sheriff.'

'Only one sheriff. I'm not obliged to them all. Anyway, it's a stupid question, I admit – I know perfectly well you loathe him.'

'I'll not deny it. But what's that to you?'

'I thought maybe I could be of help.'

'Help? How do you mean?'

'Well, I was thinking you might perhaps like to get back at him.'

'Maybe. What precisely did you have in mind?'

She rode up closer. Her knee knocked softly against his.

'Do you know where Gudjón's gone?'

'Gudjón Pálsson? Of course – everyone knows that.'

'Well, your Pétur's planning to get that girl to give false evidence. He's quite set his heart on it. So he'd be absolutely furious if she couldn't make it. Do you follow me?'

'Oh, I think I've a good enough idea. Nobody wants to see their man shown up . . .'

'Now just you listen! I'm talking about stopping false evidence – nothing else. But wouldn't you like to see his face when she doesn't appear in court? To know that everything he's worked for has failed. Wouldn't you like that?'

'I'd like that just fine. But it'd not be easy. You'd need to make it worth my while.'

She reached into her pocket and drew out a large silver brooch.

'It's pure silver. See, it comes in two like this. Here, take this one – you can have the other half when you get back. And don't think of doing anything silly – I'd simply say you stole it.'

'Right. But Gudjón doesn't ride slowly. I'm going to have to go like the devil if I'm to get there first.'

'Not if you go the other way, up over the edge of the Ódádahraun.'

'You must be mad, woman! At this time of year!'

'It'd certainly be hard going, I admit. But it's the only way. I'm sure a real man could do it.'

Thórarinn looked angrily at her and rode off.

*　　*　　*

The farm of Efraskard at which the trial was to take place stood some five miles to the north of Höskuldsstadasel. Three days before the trial was due to start, Hans kissed his wife and son goodbye and rode away to his brother-in-law's house. From the moment he left, Gudrún sat anxiously by the window, watching the ford, her throat dry and the silence weighing on her mind.

That first day no news arrived. Nor, indeed, did any come the following morning. But early in the afternoon, just as she was beginning to think that she could no longer stand the waiting, she caught sight of Einar riding back towards the river from the other side of the valley. She saw the small secretary come at full speed towards the ford and, without slowing, set his horse into the water at a furious pace, kicking up curtains of spray. As he turned for Hjardarhlíd, Gudrún hurried out to meet him.

Einar was scarcely able to speak as he dismounted.

'Sunnefa . . . !' he gasped. 'Sunnefa's dead!'

'Dead?' cried Gudrún, biting her hand. 'How?'

'I don't know exactly. Gudjón and the men from Land got back to Hvannabrekka early this morning. I was just riding along to the farms when I happened to come up with one of them. He told me that Sunnefa was dead, that she'd died just a matter of days before Gudjón arrived. I asked him how it'd happened but he said that he wasn't from Glúmsstadir itself and didn't know the details. Apparently though, Jón went quite quiet when they first told him – and then completely berserk. They had to keep him tied up all the way back east, which didn't make things too easy, what with fording the rivers. As it was, he just threw himself off his horse at one of the worst fords and it was only because they had ropes on him that they got him out. After that, the man said, it was just as if he'd completely given up . . .'

*　　*　　*

They brought Jón to Efraskard the following day. People came to their doors to see the giant of a man ride slowly by, flanked by his escort. Already the word had got round that Sunnefa was dead; and Gudrún would have been shaken if she had heard what people were saying about how Hans must have had a hand in this suspiciously sudden end to the case against him. Most of those who put forward this idea, however, were persuaded by their respect for the sheriff to conclude that he must have had it done so as to spare her a dreadful end in the Drowning Pool.

While there had always been the inevitable element of censure and moral outrage in the local attitude towards the incest of Jón and his sister, the people now found these feelings overwhelmed by those of pity for this man, who had been the victim of such great injustice. Since Jón had been sent to Smyrlabjörg, the families of Fljótsdalur had thought of the case purely in terms of Hans and his future; and real concern for either Sunnefa or Jón had become merely something reserved for discussion during the long winter evenings. But now, with the girl dead – and, as some said, prematurely – and with Jón once more in their midst, broken and useless in spite of his massive physique, they considered the seventeen years during which, through mismanagement and dilatory behaviour, the law had held him in custody; and they were angry with indignation. Being unwilling to lay the blame at Hans's feet, they looked elsewhere for a scapegoat. The only other authority they knew was Pétur; but how could that man, dour and eccentric as he was, be the cause of all those years of injustice? No, the fault must surely lie beyond – with the senior magistrates, the deputy governors, the governor himself, maybe even the powers in Denmark: all either Danes, or even worse, men in the pockets of the Danes. And as they watched the prisoner being led by, the farmers silently cursed their oppressors, just as they had done on so many occasions before.

The sitting of the court at Efraskard the next day was brief. Pétur, looking drawn and ill, rode over early in the morning, accompanied by Sigurdur Stefánsson, who had been at Hvannabrekka for the past few days. They had sat up half the night while Pétur tried to find some new line of prosecution for Sigurdur. But Sigurdur had shown little enthusiasm for the idea and kept pointing out to Pétur that, with Sunnefa's death, the case for the prosecution was over. The plaintiff, as it were, was dead. And, as far as Sigurdur was concerned, this surprise casualty was a sheer stroke of luck since it extricated him from having to explain exactly why he had achieved so little in his investigations. He wanted no new ideas of prosecution . . .

'Look, damn you!' said Pétur eventually. 'Can't you see that if Sheriff Wium isn't found guilty, Jón will be condemned?'

'So?' replied Sigurdur.

'So . . . so you'll lose a good worker for a start,' said Pétur deviously.

'That's true,' mused the man. 'Well, I've had the best part of fourteen years' free work out of him. I can't really complain. Good things can't last for ever, you know.'

Pétur stared at Sigurdur in fury.

'But he must not be allowed to get away with this! He must not, I say!' he burst out.

'That's what this is all about, isn't it?' sneered Sigurdur. 'Well, my friend, you can do your own dirty work from now on. I've had enough!'

'And what about all the money I've paid you?' answered the other man, shaking with rage.

'What about it? Try telling the court that you've been attempting to bribe me—and a lot of good that'd do you and your petty little squabble with Hans Wium. In any case,' he said yawning, 'I'd simply deny I'd ever received a thing from you . . .'

That morning, the court opened with Jón Sigurdsson reading a short letter from Angantýr, which related how Sunnefa had been unwell for a long time and how, finally, she had been found dead one morning, while she and some other women were up at the shieling. The court agreed that with the girl dead, the accusation against Hans could no longer be substantiated, unless completely new evidence turned up. In the circumstances, they decided to call Jón first.

As soon as the young man entered the court-room and had answered the customary questions of identification, he turned to Jón Sigurdsson and said that he would like to make a statement. Then, looking round at the silent members of the court, he told them in a few simple words that he had never loved anybody in his life other than his sister and that he openly admitted to having been the father of both her children. After the buzz of consternation had died down, Jón Sigurdsson asked him if he had made this statement without coercion.

'What I've said, I've said freely. If anything forced me, it was my love for my sister and a hatred of living. I have nothing else to say.'

After this statement, it was considered unnecessary to call either Hans or Gudjón; and Jón Sigurdsson, with the court unanimously behind him, proceeded to pronounce sentence. Jón was condemned to death. He was to be taken west to Land, where he would be kept on one of Angantýr's other farms for the few weeks that remained before the opening of the Great Assembly.

*　　*　　*

What a relief to be home again! Every time I have to ride to Thingvellir for Hans, I think to myself that it won't be as bad as I remember it. And every single time, it is just as bad, if not worse. This year, at least, there was the consolation of knowing that the Assembly would once and for all settle this wretched case; that, if nothing else, made the ride worthwhile. I don't think anybody was surprised to hear that the Assembly was considering commuting Jón's sentence to life imprisonment in Denmark. But what has been puzzling me is this strange business of the brooch . . .

We were on our way back, out on the southern edge of the Ódáda-hraun, not far from Trölladyngja and still a good three days from home, when we caught sight of something up by the edge of the glacier. Going to investigate, we saw that it was a couple of horses lying half-buried in the banks of snow that remained from the winter. There was no sign of their rider, but as I was scraping around in the snow, I came across a small saddle-bag in which I found a piece of silver filigree work.

One doesn't often see silverwork like that and as soon as I saw it, I knew what it was. It was part of a brooch which Hans's father had given to Ingibjörg on their wedding day, and which Ingibjörg had given to Gudrún. What puzzled me was why, if it'd been stolen, Gudrún had made no mention of the theft.

When I got back to Hjardarhlíd, I went in to see Hans and, having given him a report on the Assembly and Jón's trial, I handed him the brooch and explained how I'd come by it. He seemed just as surprised as me but quickly made light of the matter. But that evening, in front of me and several others, Hans spoke to Gudrún about it.

'Gudrún, you know that brooch of my mother's I was asking you about the other day?'

'What about it?' said Gudrún, looking down at her plate.

'Well, did you know that half of it was missing?'

'Missing? But how could it possibly be missing, Hans?'

'Well, it must've been because Einar's just found it,' said Hans, with his eyes on his wife.

'But how extraordinary!' said Gudrún, quite coolly – though omitting to ask where I'd discovered it.

While the matter itself soon passed out of my mind, a few days later Hans quite suddenly referred to it all again.

'Would you say there was any way of knowing in which direction the horses were travelling?'

'The horses?' I asked, completely baffled.

'Yes, the horses you found up by Trölladyngja,' he replied, looking away. 'Would you say they were on their way back from the southwest? Or were they travelling in that direction – away from Fljótsdalur?'

'Oh, those horses! Well, I couldn't really say.'

*　　*　　*

The farmer stopped Gunnar as he was passing by on his way south, saying that the young man was ill and needed attention. When Gunnar asked the farmer what seemed to be wrong, the old man shrugged.

'I really couldn't say. There's no sickness on him so far as I can tell. But he'll not live long at this rate – that I can say. He's not touched a bite in three weeks. Nothing.'

Gunnar found him in the empty hay-loft.

'Jón?' he called up softly.

Getting no answer, Gunnar climbed up and found the man lying on a thin bed of hay under the slope of the roof. He sat down opposite him and waited. A faint light filtered in through the one dirty window and as Gunnar became accustomed to the dimness, he realized that the man was staring at him.

'Jón?' he said again.

The man did not move.

'Jón, they say that you're not eating. You'll need to take something, you know. You can't go on lying there like that . . .'

His voice died away. Jón still stared at him with unflickering eyes.

'Are you the doctor?'

The hollow voice seemed not to belong to the great emaciated body.

'Yes,' he said, 'I am.'

'Well, doctor, perhaps you'll understand me better than the rest of them here. I'll be dead soon. You know that as well as I do. And when I'm gone and they fill my mouth with mud and stones, I'll be better off.'

'But Jón, man, what sense is there in that sort of talk?' protested the young doctor. 'You know that they've commuted your sentence.'

'Sense?' answered Jón dully. 'What's sense got to do with it? Now just let me be!'

155

Gunnar pursed his lips and looked up at the little patch of summer sky that showed through the window.

*　　*　　*

Later that same day, some hundred and sixty miles to the north-east, the light of the low-slung sun hung draped on the crags above Hvannabrekka. Down in the valley, the night-time half-light was settling over the buildings.

In the main room, Pétur sat at his desk. His journal lay open and the empty pages were splattered with ink from where he had cast down his quill. He was sprawled forward over the desk with his head buried in his arms. He groaned and mumbled to himself and, from time to time, his fist struck the desk-top violently.

'But why, why, father? Why, O Lord?'

*　　*　　*

In the autumn of 1757, Jón Jónsson died. His death was hardly noticed among the thousands of casualties that had occurred since the beginning of the famine; but, in Fljótsdalur, the news was received as being the long overdue ending to a scandalous case, a case that had caused unhappiness and bad feeling in the district for nearly two decades. At Hjardarhlíd, Gudrún and Einar were openly relieved – as were Eiríkur and Gudný at Höskuldsstadasel – but Hans himself took the news badly. At Hvannabrekka, Gudjón, as usual, seemed totally indifferent to the whole matter, while Pétur . . . well, there were starting to be serious rumours about the soundness of Pétur's mind.

5

HANS AND PÉTUR: 1765

The March wind came fast across the open stretches of high moorland, where fields of snow and ice had blotted out rock and marsh and heather. It peeled away over the edge of the heights and descended on the Lagarfljót and the farms of Fljótsdalur, flaying any bush-top or sliver of black stream-water that lay in its path. The snow clouds ran low and gave the slash of the Lagarfljót a dull, blue-grey gleam; but otherwise this white, secluded world was stained only by the occasional farm, where a coil of smoke, a dark doorway or a cluster of horses showed up in the flat light.

From time to time, squalls of snow broke out, swarms of flakes creating a dense chaos that obscured everything. But this did not seem to deter the two horsemen who were just setting out from Hjardarhlíd and heading down towards the ford. They rode side by side and both of them carried short swords.

That winter's day, Einar was seeing Niels Wium over to the other side of the Lagarfljót for his studies with the minister. Soon to be fifteen, Niels had kept his mother's looks but, having added some of his father's height, now had a certain adolescent awkwardness to him. With the disappointments and frustrations of his own career, Hans, together with Gudrún, had now turned all his interest on to the boy; and so the family at Hjardarhlíd these days, in which the loyal Einar was included, was a strong, closely-knit affair.

As they rode along side by side, heavily muffled against the weather, the boy was laughing and turning his horse about as the small storms of snow blew up around them. At the ford, Einar found a way down through the drifts and, leading the boy's horse, set out into the water. Halfway over, a sudden blasting turbulence announced another snow squall and Einar shouted back at the boy to keep close.

It was as they came up out of the river, leaning into the soft grapeshot of the squall, that the horseman appeared. He rose as if from nowhere, right up above them, a figure wrapped in sheepskin and carrying a sword. He rode down hard on them, knocking Einar aside and ripping away the reins of Niels's horse. Einar drew his sword and swung at him, but steel met steel, and the next moment

157

a heavy, backhanded blow with the pommel had sent the small man senseless into the snow.

When he staggered back to his feet, there was only his own horse, standing head down to the battering wind. As he rode up the bank, the squall passed on and light came back into the sky. But though he shouted at the top of his voice time and again, there was no sign either of Niels or the horseman. Riding back, he found tracks and quickly followed them down along the river's edge, a growing apprehension now gripping him. When they led up on to a rocky overhang in a bend of the river, he suddenly knew, and shouted out the boy's name once, twice in a voice broken by horror. And there from the rock he saw it: straight below him, the ragged hole in the whiteness of ice, where the dark waters showed slurrying past.

'No, no, no!' he mouthed, dizzy and sickened, as he turned to climb down.

A while later, a short way downstream, he knelt bent on the bank, clutching the frozen body, and closed his eyes against the impossible vision of death. Then, hauling the sodden child on to the horse, he prepared to ride back to Hjardarhlíd where he had left Hans and Gudrún talking by the fire.

*　　*　　*

Gunnlaug Kjartansdóttir, Pétur's foster-mother, sat knitting at Hvannabrekka. As the heavy needles clacked and chattered, her mouth ceaselessly ruminated and a toneless tune rose from the back of her throat. Toothless and addle-headed, she carried her sixty-seven years poorly: now, beyond being dimly annoyed that Pétur should have chosen to be away, she was drifting easily in her state of dotage. And even when a violent battering sound at the outside door was heard above the noise of the storm, her equanimity remained quite untroubled. Pétur would not be back for a few days: the arrival of anybody else was of no great interest to her.

But then the door of the room was almost taken from its hinges as the man burst in.

'Now who are you?' she asked the snow-covered man standing before her.

'Where is he?' hissed Hans. 'Where's Pétur?'

158

'I don't think I know you, do I?' she chuckled, 'If you only knew how funny you looked.' She went off into a peal of giggles.

'Old mother!' said the man, striding over and seizing her arm. 'Now you listen to me. I'm asking where that smug bastard is, that Pétur Thorsteinsson, who acts the good sheriff and who's no more than a vicious hypocrite, a perverted monster. Where is he, mother? Tell me fast or I'll crush the life from you – just as he crushed the life from my boy.'

The old woman stared sulkily at her knitting and shrugged.

'How should I know what you're talking about?'

'Where . . . is . . . Pétur?' screamed Hans into her ear.

The old woman looked slyly up at him.

'Away,' she said.

Hans released her arm in disgust and went over to the desk. Taking paper and pen, he began to write.

'I'm serving a writ for murder on Pétur and that man of his, Gudjón Pálsson,' he said without looking up; but the woman had already gone back to her knitting.

Although Pétur returned to Hvannabrekka at the end of the week, Gudjón Pálsson was never to be seen again in Fljótsdalur. Hans himself came home from Hvannabrekka that day with his crazed grief already falling away into dejection and misery. But then, as the days of waiting passed, the numbed pain of his loss brought up a cold hatred in him. And so, as soon as he heard that Pétur was back, he put on his Sunday clothes, saddled his best horse and rode at a measured pace up Sudurdalur to the farm that crouched under the high, snow-packed hills.

'So what's this?' Pétur said aggressively, waving the writ at Hans as he came in.

'Just exactly what it says,' replied Hans in a stony voice. 'Last Monday, my son was murdered. I intend making sure that you pay for it. In full.'

'Don't you try and bluff me, you pompous fool! I've been over at Kirkjulækur with Haraldur Bödvarsson since Sunday last so you'll not manage to blame it on me like that. Anyway, what's all this about murder? I heard the boy just got drowned . . .'

'Don't start trying to tell me what happened, damn you!' said Hans. 'My son and Einar were attacked at the ford and . . . and the boy killed – if not actually by you, then on your orders. God knows, it'd be simpler if I were just to cut your throat here and now as you deserve. But that's not what I want. I'm going to make sure you admit to it all in public.'

'Ha! And what exactly do you think you're going to be able to pin on me then?' said Pétur, his eyes starting from his head. 'When this . . . this thing happened, I was thirty miles away at Kirkjulækur. Haraldur will vouch for that. And as for what Gud . . .'

'Go on,' said Hans, suddenly very calm, as the man's voice trailed away. 'Go on – finish what you were saying.'

'You're trying to trip me up, you devil!' screamed the man, beating his knuckles on the desk. 'You are, you are!'

'So you got Gudjón to do it, didn't you, you scum? You set that fat beast on a young, innocent boy, a boy who was kind and generous and . . .'

'Shut up!' howled the other man like an angry child. 'Don't you try and smear my name with the kind of filth for which your family is known. I won't have it! I won't!'

'There's never been a murderer in my family, I'll have you know – let alone a murderer who masquerades as a paragon of piety. You revolt me!'

'Never been a murderer in your family, hasn't there?' said Pétur, quite suddenly turning cool and snake-like. 'And just how did Sunnefa Jónsdóttir die then? And what about her brother's death? Neither of these would've happened if you hadn't been such a coward and had admitted your crime. Isn't that murder? And as if that weren't enough for one family to have suffered at the hands of you bloody Danish Wiums, what about their mother? What about your father, that criminal maniac who thought nothing of slaughtering a defenceless woman? Eh? What about that, I ask you? And you can stand there and say there's never been a murderer in your family! Pah!'

Pétur's voice had gradually risen to a shriek again.

'What do you mean?' asked Hans through his teeth. 'What are you saying about my father?'

'Ha, ha!' laughed Pétur with wide, bright eyes of triumph. 'You didn't know about that, did you? You didn't realize what a degenerate toad it was that begot you, did you now?'

Sticking out his chest and chin, he burst into shrill laughter. Hans stepped forward and seized him by his jacket.

'By God, I'll silence your smutty mouth for good! I'll not have you peddling your lies about the countryside.'

'Lies, Hans? That's no lie,' said the man flatly, making no attempt to free himself and smiling superciliously at Hans. 'I learnt it from Jón Jónsson himself. Have you never wondered at the way in which he and Sunnefa hated you? But come now, think back a bit, Hans . . . Spring 1733? Why, you must have been about eighteen . . . Don't you remember your father coming home from Seydisfjördur a bit the worse for wear, having drunk himself sick and lost most of the revenues?'

Hans gripped him more fiercely. He felt a sudden urge to kill the man: but, at the same time, he felt his anger paralysed by a horrible fascination for the words that spilled from Pétur's mouth. Hideous memories and half-memories were rising to the surface of his mind.

'Yes,' said Pétur, sensing his advantage. 'Yes, that's right, it was in the spring of 1733, when your noble father had gone north with a handful of men to sell the produce in Seydisfjördur . . .'

★   ★   ★

The sheriff reined in his horse and squinted up at the sun. His fleshy face was red from the sharp wind and the brandy that he had been drinking ever since leaving Seydisfjördur soon after dawn. He had ridden slowly along the edge of the fjord, leaving the main cluster of houses still buried in shadows, and had then turned north up through the mountains, where a track led over to Lodmundarfjördur and on to Borgarfjördur.

As he sat there in the sunlight and stared down at the polished plate of the North Atlantic, he smirked at the thought of his companions from Fljótsdalur who were now riding home, having offered to carry the money back with them for safety's sake. The poor fools! Jens knew that the only time money was safe was when it was in your own pocket. And – God! – the thought of riding straight home to Hjardarhlíd where there was nothing to greet him but Ingibjörg's silent criticism and the sour looks of the children . . . Well, perhaps there was no way of escaping that for ever but, by Christ, he'd give himself a few days of fun with Brønsted first!

Jens laughed at the thought of his compatriot up in Borgarfjördur. Now there was a man who'd got his life well organized – a good business but nobody to answer to except some man miles away in Denmark; no wife but a good-looking woman to do for him and to share his bed when the mood took him; one or two Danish friends in the area but no stupid ideas of trying to mix with the damned Icelanders . . . Yes, Brønsted was right – stay out here for a few years, make what the traders liked to call 'a bit of cash' and then go home for good.

Jens thought of his own prospects and quickly had another pull at the flask. He sat there frowning, his eyes watering as the wind slashed down from the ridge. Far out over the fjord, a sea-eagle stalked along the cliffs where the surf grew thick upon the rocks . . . No, it was better to drink than to think. He took another draught.

He was drunk when he reached Brønsted's house and drunk when he left it, three days later. But Jens was a man who held his liquor well and although the consumption of brandy had been heavy during those days, he sat steadily enough on his horse as he rode away from the house and went along the shore of the fjord.

As always, the drinking had awoken anger and resentment in him. The alcohol had not only increased his awareness of his own isolation but had also induced a strange state of mental clarity in which he saw his life in true perspective. He was trapped. The way back – to Denmark – was closed to him; the way forward – a continuation of his present life with Ingibjörg and the children – was still open yet he felt that it could only lead to a distant dead-end. Jens was intelligent enough to know that he had failed. The only thing in which he had succeeded was the making of money. Money and always more money – but never enough to assuage that sense of failure. And now, in the remote vacuum created by his intoxication, he felt a formless but urgent desire to prove himself again, to pit himself against the world just as he had dreamed of doing as a young man in Copenhagen. Had he had his chance or was there still time?

When he had reached the mouth of the fjord and was about to turn west for the way home, he dismounted by a small stream and knelt down to drink. It was as he was crouching there that a sudden noise made him turn. A hundred yards away, the door of an old turf building opened and a young woman walked out. She caught sight of Jens and his horses but turned away towards a farm that stood further along the hillside.

'Hey, you there!' called the sheriff, standing up.

The woman stopped and looked round. Jens mounted and rode over to her.

'What do they call you?' said Jens, looking down at the woman.

162

She was tall, with an angular, white face and brown eyes. She was perhaps a year or two over thirty. Her long upper lip curled slightly as she answered.

'I tell my name to those I choose,' she said.

Jens laughed.

'Do you know who I am?' he asked.

'No. But I can hear you're Danish. And now, if you'll excuse me, I'll be on my way. I've better things to do than stand and chat with foreigners.'

As she stepped out, Jens rode his horse in front of her.

'You still haven't told me your name.'

'And I suppose you'll let me pass if I do,' she said sarcastically.

'I might,' he said. 'Try me.'

'My name's Gudbjörg.'

'And where's your man, Gudbjörg?'

'Dead,' she answered flatly. 'Now let me go.'

But now a smile had appeared on his face. He rode his horse slowly at her. Although she was too proud to let her fear show, she was forced to retreat down the slope by the advancing animal.

'Stop it!' she cried eventually.

But it was as if he did not hear her. He came relentlessly on. He watched her breathing quicken, the tightening of her eyes, the little frown appearing on her forehead. And then, as she suddenly realized what was going to happen, she turned and ran for the little turf house. He caught up with her just as she reached it; but before he could seize her, she had leapt inside and was trying to bolt the door. Jens sprang from his horse and threw himself against the door which burst open, knocking the woman across the room.

He locked the door behind him. But when he turned, he found himself facing the barbed head of a shark-harpoon.

'Come on, this is stupid,' he said with a laugh. 'It'll get us nowhere at all.'

'Get out!' she said in a low voice.

He saw the way the harpoon trembled and walked confidently towards her with his hand out.

'Put it down, woman, or you'll regret it,' he said sternly.

But instead, she lunged at him. He jumped aside with a curse as the barb ripped his hand.

'God damn you, you bitch!' he said and sprang at her, seizing her arm.

163

She twisted and turned to escape him, feeling his arms come round her from behind and try to wrench the weapon from her grip. He had managed to pull it round towards him when she stumbled and they both fell heavily to the ground. She screamed out; and, as he tried to free himself, he felt something prod him in the groin. Looking down, he saw the harpoon's barb protruding from her back.

He seized up his flask which had spilt all over the floor. The woman meanwhile lay doubled up and groaning, with her thin white hands clasping the root of the dark shaft that sprouted from her belly. He tore open the door and ran for his horse. At that very moment, a shout sounded out from up at the farm; but, without bothering to look back, he mounted and went like a hawk for the hills.

★   ★   ★

Some local men calling at Hvannabrekka on business and hearing shouts, broke in and separated the two men. Pétur, although no shorter than Hans, had grown as weak in his body as he had in his mind over the past years and was no match for Hans's furious strength. When the farmers pulled Hans off him, they found that he had several wounds from Hans's knife. As they carried him away to his bed, he looked up at Hans.

'I shall stand over your dead body if it's the last thing I do,' he whispered.

Hans turned away and spat.

A SECOND EPILOGUE: 1788

They sat close together by the little pile of smouldering turf and dung that acted as a fire. He kept rolling his head from side to side and massaging his temples with the tips of his fingers, while she stared at the fitful flames and hugged her knees.

'Forty-eight years!' he said, half to himself. 'It's almost a lifetime.'

The wind drove blunt tines of rain against the window. The darkness of the night came into the room and encased them, right down to the small flush of light which spilt from the smoking lamp.

'But Sólrún,' said the white-haired man in a tremulous voice, 'I

164

need you to tell me about it. How you've lived out this half-century while I believed you dead. I need to form a picture of it so that I can feel that in some way I've lived it too. I don't want to think that life has entirely passed me by.'

She glanced at him and laid her hand on his arm.

'Pétur, at least don't fret on my account,' she said gently. 'I've had my life and if it was not quite what I'd hoped for as a young girl, it was certainly better than it might well have been. Isn't that how it is for most people? Shouldn't we just be thankful for what we were spared – rather than dwelling on what we feel we were denied? Anyway, I came back. I never forgot. And now we shall stay together.

'Well,' she began, 'you know how it was that day – bright and beautiful. Just the day for a ride over to Haugar, I thought. Anyway, I was halfway down the valley when all of a sudden Jón Bjarnason appeared from behind a rock; and without so much as a word, seized my reins and began to lead me away up the hill. I cried out and struck at him but he merely threatened to cut my throat if I didn't keep quiet.

'I was terrified. I was fairly sure what he had in mind – but when we came out on top, I saw to my surprise that there was another rider, waiting with some other horses out on the skyline. As we drew nearer, I saw that this was Jens Wium. Reaching him, we all set off at a fast pace; and, by now, I was really scared because I had no idea what was happening. In fact, I soon couldn't stand it any longer and cried out to Jens, asking why he was torturing me, why he didn't just finish me off there and then. He laughed and told me to stop my mewling, saying that he had no intention of harming me as he was going to make me his wife. I began to cry at this. Wasn't one wife enough for him? And anyway, wife or no wife, why were we riding out into the wilderness like this? But though they both laughed, they didn't give me an answer.

'We spent that night in a bothy. I don't ever remember being so cold. Jens sat up, writing by the light of a little travelling-lamp while I could only lie there shivering under the rugs, listening to the blizzard outside and wondering what was to become of me.

'When we set off the next day, the moon was still up. The snow had stopped but the wind was whipping across the hills. I honestly thought I'd die in that wind. But as dawn began to appear, we rode down off the heights and joined the track under Öxi, which we followed through to Berufjördur. There we went to a farmhouse where there were two men who undertook to row us out in their boat. By now, I was beginning to think that I was being taken to some remote farm down the coast – but as we rounded the headland, I saw a large ship at anchor. Perhaps we were going away to the west fjords, I thought, to somewhere where we couldn't be found.

'Then, as we drew near the ship, I suddenly saw that Jens had drawn a dagger. He was behind the two rowers, up in the bows, and when I saw what was going to happen, I started up. But Jón held me back while Jens killed the two men. A short while later, we were on board the ship and were pulling away from the coast.

'Hearing the sailors talking in a foreign language, I asked Jens where we were going.

'"To Scotland!" he cried. "To a new life!"

'A new life! Down in the cabin, I couldn't stop the tears when I thought of you and realized that I'd never see you again. I thought of how I was going to spend my life married to a man I didn't love, who was thirty years older than me and who was a Dane at that. And of how I should live and die among people whom I couldn't understand, whose customs and whole way of life would be strange and unsympathetic to me, how . . . Well, as you can imagine, at that moment I just wished I were dead . . .

'We were at sea for more than ten days but I remember little of the voyage other than my misery and the fear I felt as we laboured in heavy seas south of the Faroes. Later, a south-westerly delayed us by driving us back north towards Shetland but eventually we reached our destination, a little port on the northernmost coast of the Scottish mainland. From there, we travelled inland until Jens found what he wanted, a small farm near a place in Caithness named Vatn – or Watten as the Scots call it. It seemed a good enough farm to me; but after a couple of years, Jens was looking for something bigger and so we moved across to the east coast, to a large farm near the mouth of the river Brora or, as we say, Brúará. By that time, Jón Bjarnason was no longer with us. About eighteen months after we arrived, he and Jens quarrelled and Jón went off on his own.

'But for all that he'd kidnapped me and forced a life on me that I'd never have chosen, it'd only be fair to say that Jens was always kind and considerate to me, and I never lacked for anything. And it was an easier life over there, in Scotland – the winters weren't so harsh, there was plenty of fuel, and the earth was good, bearing barley and oats, potatoes and kale. After those first, miserable months, I suppose I got by simply by putting all thoughts of you and home out of my mind. And then things changed when my children were born – my son, Niall, in '44 and my daughter, Margaret, two years after. Of course, by now they're both long grown up and with families of their own: Niall married a fisherman's daughter – they're living in a town not far from Brora, where he's a merchant. Margaret's husband is Norwegian, a corn chandler, and they're away to the south. I haven't seen so much of them since they married but they're both well settled and I'm happy for them.

'Our life at the farm was good. The people round about were friendly enough and Jens did well with the cattle. There was one period though, just after Niall was born, when we heard terrible stories about the soldiers coming up from England to crush the people just to the south of us, who'd been forced to carry arms for some king or other from abroad. But as we then heard that the king in England was himself a foreigner, from Germany, it was all bit hard to understand.

'But while Jens did so well and was good enough to me, I have to admit he always remained something of an enigma. I don't think he was really capable of warmth, or even of properly sharing his life with me. And he never spoke about the past, either of Iceland or Denmark – it was just as if he had no memory of anything before that day in Sudurdalur. I think he was secretly unhappy about it all, though he never said so to me.

'I remember hearing stories about his drinking when I lived at Hvannabrekka. But from the day we arrived in Scotland, I never saw him touch a drop. And then, quite suddenly, all those years later, when he was an old man in his eighties, he took to the whisky, which is the local drink there. When I tried to talk to him about it, he would just go off and shut himself away in his room. Finally, one night a few weeks before his ninetieth birthday, there came the most terrible noise from his room. He was shouting and screaming in Danish and battering at the door as if trying to escape. But the door was locked from the inside; and, for all that I called out to him, I couldn't make him understand that he must open it for us. And then, quite suddenly, silence. Later, when we'd broken the door down, we found him lying dead, with his face contorted and his tongue purple and half-bitten through. It was a horrible sight and one I'll never forget. As soon as I'd buried him, I sold the farm and went to live with Niall and his family.

'I was fifty-eight when Jens died. I still felt young – perhaps from having lived with a man so much older than myself – but after a while I began to realize that I was, in fact, too old to start again. And then I looked at Niall and his family and realized that, son of mine though he was, he had his own life and that anyway I didn't want to die in his house. It was at about that time that I began to dream of this valley again, vivid dreams of you and this house which seemed to be empty and cold. The vividness of the dreams was quite disturbing, considering I'd heard nothing of you in forty years. I didn't even know if you were still alive . . . And yet I knew that I had to come home. All those years abroad hadn't stopped me thinking of Iceland as home. I had to come back . . .

'Late in 1782, I went down south to say goodbye to Margaret. I stayed there a while and then returned to Niall to wait for a boat. A few months later, the first news of the Skaftá Fires reached us; and not long afterwards, the ash and the black cloud confirmed what we'd heard. Niall forbade me to go back – even if I could find a boat to take me – until I could convince him that it'd be safe. It was to be more than four years before we heard that the worst of the fires and famine and pestilence were over – but all this you know rather better than I do. So it wasn't until three weeks ago that I finally said goodbye to my son and his family and put to sea . . .'

The fire had come alive and its little flames scattered brightness over the tears that ran on the old man's furrowed face.

'I just can't bear to think of it,' he said, 'the way that man took your life and used it. He may have given you a home and comfort – but he also destroyed what you really were. Christ Almighty, I'd have killed him with my bare hands if I'd known what he was going to do . . .'

Sólrún leant forward and poked at the fire.

'Hans Wium!' Pétur whispered to himself, his eyes cold and staring.

'What's that?' she said, turning to him.

But the man was already far away again; and the wind and rain were weaving a chill, impenetrable web about the house as the night hours marched resolutely on towards the coming dawn.

*   *   *

'I wonder . . .' said Einar.

It was half-past four in the morning. They had been talking all night and the little room was thick with pipe-smoke, though this did not serve to camouflage the sweet horrors of putrefying flesh that hung in the air. Next door, the patient was silent, his mind dulled by the dose of chloral which the doctor had given him an hour before, when the secondary fever had broken out. The man had begun to struggle and cry out, making a horrible croaking that was the result of the disease's ravages in his mouth and throat. In spite of the distortions of his voice, it was clear to the two men that in his delirium he was calling for his wife and son. It was twenty-three years since that white, wild day when Niels had died in the river; and at least fifteen since Gudrún, weakened by misery, had finally been seized away by pneumonia one still night in the dead of winter. Hans's incessant and raucous cries had been so unbearable that, even after Gunnar had administered the drug, the two men had fallen into a state of dejection. Little by little, Gunnar had begun to drop off and he had been almost asleep when Einar's voice plucked him back awake.

'What do you wonder?' said Gunnar, yawning and lighting his pipe.

Einar rubbed his nose and stared thoughtfully at the floor.

'Well, I was just thinking about the strange way in which Hans caught this filthy thing. What would you say?'

'I really don't know, Einar. But what's certain is that he must've come in contact with some person or object, somewhere in the region of three to four weeks ago.'

'Hmmm . . .' said Einar, deep in thought. 'An object? Like a piece of clothing or something?'

'Yes, an infected garment could certainly have caused it.'

Einar told Gunnar the story of the shirt that Hans had found in his bed.

'Nobody else knew anything about it and Hans himself threw it straight on to the fire in the morning.'

'But it's all a bit far-fetched, isn't it? I mean, who would actually go to all the trouble of smuggling in something like that and putting it under his pillow?'

The men looked at each other for a moment, then fell silent once more.

Gradually the night passed away. Once the sun came rising into the sky, it was as if the resurgence of life-giving light symbolized the end of the vigil, as if the dying man suddenly sensed that his mere survival of that long night signified the final triumph of courage over suffering and so gave him his release.

He called out weakly to Gunnar and began to talk to him about his burial.

'And Gunnar . . .' Einar heard, as the exhausted voice rasped slowly on the dawn silence. 'I've only one request about my burial . . .'

'Yes?'

'That he should not be present.'

'Who?'

'You know – that man!' whispered Hans hoarsely. 'Haven't I paid enough already – for my father's wrongs and for my own failings. It's not right that he should be allowed to rejoice again, in my death.

'You see, the lie about the girl was somehow of his making. A lie to destroy me. I knew it. I always knew it but just couldn't prove it . . .

'Tell Einar to take my old green coat to Hvannabrekka with a message from me. Tell him to say that I leave it to the man who borrowed it from me before – that day up at Axlir. It's of no importance that I shall never know who wears it . . .'

Two hours later, Hans was dead. The end was quiet and undramatic. Standing in the doorway, Einar gazed for a few moments at the horribly disfigured corpse and then turned away. As he wandered out of the house into the cool morning sunshine, the picture left in his mind was a sad mockery of the powerful, spirited sheriff he remembered from fifty years before. In fact, Einar thought to himself, virtually the only things that remained of the original man were the big silver ring and the unbending refusal to compromise.

*   *   *

The two brothers cursed loudly as they worked. They were both covered in mud and their hands were cold and raw as they hacked open the rocky ground.

'It's no bloody fun doing this sort of work at the best of times. But when you're asked for a grave of this size and told that it's got to be ready in a couple of hours, you'd think that the Almighty would consider holding off the bad weather, wouldn't you? Some

170

bloody hope!' grumbled one of them as the rain cut him across the face. 'Anyway, let's hope that this one's the last of the smallpox victims. It's all very well for the minister to say that the grave needs to be an extra foot deeper for a poxy body . . . but I'd like to see his fat little face if he had to dig that deep.'

'Oh, for Christ's sake, Stefán, stop your bellyaching and get on with it! It'll not be long before they arrive and they'll hardly bless us if they have to stand around in this weather while we finish the job.'

'All right, all right!' said Stefán, wiping some mud from his eye and glancing angrily at his brother. 'But it'd serve them right all the same.'

By now, they were down in the grave, and the rain, which fell in torrents, was kicking up gouts of mud and sending fat rivulets of water over the edge of the hole, turning the earth into a quagmire. It was just before they had finished that Stefán suddenly stopped, halfway through a swing of his spade, and hissed at his brother.

'Hey! Who in the hell's that?'

'Where?'

'Just over there, on the horse! Christ, he gave me a hell of a fright! He's wearing Sheriff Wium's coat. God in heaven! Do you see who it is? The man must be as mad as they say he is . . . Listen – let's get done and get out of here before the burial party arrives. I really don't fancy being here when they see him.'

A few minutes later, they clambered out of the grave and made their way down towards their horses that were tethered behind the church. As they passed the man in the green coat, Stefán could not stop himself looking up.

'Good afternoon, Pétur!' he said nervously. But he got no acknowledgement from the man, who sat motionless on his horse and stared with a look of bitter amusement at the muddy hole in the earth.

6

A POSTSCRIPT

On a sudden impulse, I get down from my horse and plunge my face into the waters of a mountain stream. The blackness of the story has taken its toll of me and I'm shaking with a strange exhaustion. The little pool is alive with young sunlight and a prehistoric coldness; and as I sink my head into it, my whole world is filled by its embrace and the thrumming of a small waterfall just above me. Oh God, and I shall soon be dead!, I think to myself. There's more in the touch of cold water than in the hopes and dreams of half a lifetime . . . As I surface again and blink my way back to the world, the new day touches at my old man's face and strings my eyelashes with such uncontrollable fire and brightness that I'm quite suddenly overcome. Old fool that I am! I shake my head and laugh. There – I say to myself – there, now it's gone! The moment has passed! Surely I'm too old for such things . . .

I went back to where Kjartan was waiting with the horses.

'It's not far now,' he said. 'You'll be at Audnir within the hour.'

I remounted and we rode on.

But, about a mile before we came to his home at Bakki, Kjartan suddenly brought the subject up again.

'But there's still so much to be guessed at, Gunnar, isn't there? By inference, one suspects the part that Pétur played; but the state of his mind upsets the simple reasoning of the matter. His behaviour at Hans's burial, the entries in his journal that you were shown . . . and even the accusations that Hans himself made before he died – all these things could only too easily lead one to believe that Pétur was both more evil and more insane than he was judged to be during his lifetime. But it strikes me that it's all open to doubt, that the evidence is cumulative rather than definite.'

'Quite so,' I replied. 'But, in fact, there was one other thing that I learnt much later, a long time after Hans's death . . .

'One by one, the people who'd had a part in the story died off. Sólrún in '89, Eiríkur in '90 and, in 1791, Gudný, Einar and Pétur himself – none of them young by then. By the end of that year, it really seemed as though the story was closed once and for all.

'But a full ten years later, in 1800, I was called over to the farm of Thverárkot to attend to an old woman who'd fallen and broken her leg. I can't recall her name but it's of no importance. Anyway, the weather that day was rough and when I'd set the leg and made sure she was comfortable, the woman's brother, an old man called Adalsteinn, suggested that I stay the night.

'Now Adalsteinn was a man whom I scarcely knew for he'd been away in Norway for the greater part of his life, living as a fisherman in the Lofoten Islands, and had only returned to his family's farm a couple of years before. Late that night, when the others had gone to bed, we sat together by the fire, drinking coffee and smoking our pipes.

'He told me how, at the age of seventeen, he'd quarrelled with his father and his elder brother about the future of the farm – and so he'd resolved to leave. Rather than try and find a place elsewhere in the district, he'd decided to go abroad. It was in May 1741 that he finally sailed east and began his life in Norway.

'It was an interesting enough story that he had to tell me about his life in the islands and I listened without interrupting him. When, however, he'd finished and we were sitting thoughtfully over the dying fire, he suddenly turned to a new subject.

'"What finally happened to that man, the sheriff at Hvannabrekka . . . Pétur Thorsteinsson?"

'"Good heavens!" I replied, "did you know him? He died some nine or ten years ago."

'"Ah, did he . . . ? Well," he said, "I never had that much to do with him, as I was still only a youngster when I left the country, as I told you. It was just that the last time I saw him was in rather strange circumstances."

'"Really?" I asked, my curiosity aroused.

'"Yes. I'll tell you if you like . . ."'

*   *   *

Late one afternoon in April of the year in which I left the country, news came through to Thverárkot that a man had been lost, up on the marshes to the north of Fljótsdalur; and that a search party was being organized for the next morning. Both my father and my brother were busy but I was only too glad of an excuse to get away – so I volunteered to join the searchers.

Early the following day, I rode away down to the ford and met

173

up with the men from the other farms. We made our way from there up onto the marshes where it was decided that we should split up into groups of three and work over the ground between Fljótsdalur and Brú. This sounded a fairly simple operation but it was to prove otherwise for the mist up there that morning was incredibly thick.

The groups were chosen, and I and another lad of my age were put in the charge of Pétur Thorsteinsson from Hvannabrekka, who'd joined the party at the last moment. Our group was given the most westerly station, right on the edge of the marshes; and Pétur decided that while I was to be in the middle and the other boy on my right, he himself would ride out on our left – which made him the furthest west of the whole party.

We set off and it soon became clear that we were going to have our work cut out merely to keep contact with each other. In places, visibility was down to a few feet and, what with the pools and patches of bog, it was difficult to keep to a fixed course. In these conditions, two riders only twenty paces apart were virtually in separate worlds. But we pressed on, occasionally calling out to each other, and soon enough we were out near the middle of the marshes.

It was about an hour or so after we'd started that Pétur startled me by suddenly appearing by my side from out of the mist. He told me that he was going to take a look right over in the corner of the marshes where they ran up under the hills and that I wasn't to worry if I didn't see him for a while. When I pointed out that nobody travelling to Brú could possibly have wandered that far west, he just laughed and rode off.

Some time later, after I'd lost touch with the boy riding to the east of me, I found myself moving up the side of a small mound that pushed up out of the flat marshland. Coming to the top of this hillock, I discovered that it stood clear of the mist and that I could see all the hills to the west quite clearly.

Just then, I caught sight of somebody at the foot of the hills. He was about three-quarters of a mile away, up by the bothy at Axlir. My first thought was that it was one of the searchers – and I was just about to turn away when I saw another man spring out from cover and strike him fiercely over the head. This second man heaved the body on to a horse and, after placing a sack over the unconscious man's head, proceeded to strip him of his coat. Having done this, he quickly lashed the man's hands around the horse's neck and, putting on the coat, went into the bothy.

Until that moment, I hadn't managed to get a clear view of either of them; but I now saw who the attacker was. As a young man I had particularly good eyesight and there was now no doubt in my mind. It was Pétur Thorsteinsson.

I was seventeen and planning to leave the country in a month to start a new life. I didn't want any trouble. No doubt all I'd witnessed was a case of assault and robbery.

I turned my horse and rode swiftly down into the mist to catch up with the others.

Gradually the mist began to thin. The sheriff joined us for a short while a bit later, though he puzzled me still further by appearing from the south, as if he'd come from Fljótsdalur. He was silent and gloomy; and when he rode off again, saying that he had to go home, I noticed that his horse was in a lather.

For the whole of that day we combed those marshes but apart from finding, rather strangely, a single, human ear, we came across no other trace of man or beast.

Four weeks later, I sailed out of the fjords for Norway. I'd made no mention of what I'd seen to anybody.

*　　*　　*

I left Kjartan at Bakki. I watched him ride exuberantly up to the farm which stood by itself at the foot of the slopes and then turned away and went on.

The gulls were crying excitedly over the fjord and the sun's light came down through a clear sky. A breeze rocked gently about over the shore and brought the taste of salt to my lips. Audnir, my home, lay just over the hill . . .

My God, it was good to be alive!